Amy held her breath as she slid into the backseat and smiled at her blind date. "Hi, I'm Amy," she said.

"Hi, Amy. I'm Tommy." He blinked and took a second look at her. "You have a black eye."

"Yeah." *Give him two points for being observant*, she thought. Amy's best friend Laura and her date turned around from the front seat to look at her.

"Are you sure you're okay?" Laura's date asked.

Amy saw concern in his friendly brown eyes. "I'm all right. It's just a little bruise I got playing racquetball."

He offered her a crooked grin, and Amy's breath caught in her throat. Laura had told her she didn't think he was cute, but Amy thought he was adorable with his wavy, reddish brown hair and warm amber eyes. She even liked the little space that showed between his front teeth when he grinned.

"We haven't been introduced. I'm Ben Richardson." He reached his right arm over the seat to shake hands.

Amy put her mittened hand inside his bare one. "I'm Amy Tyler." *Laura's date is something else*, she thought. *I can't understand why Laura isn't more interested in him. I would be.*

Bantam Sweet Dreams Romances
Ask your bookseller for the books you have missed

Crossed Signals

Janice Boies

BANTAM BOOKS

TORONTO • NEW YORK • LONDON • SYDNEY • AUCKLAND

RL 6, IL age 11 and up

CROSSED SIGNALS
A Bantam Book/July 1990

Cover photo by Pat Hill.

ISBN 0-553-27593-3

Published simultaneously in the United States and Canada

Bantam Books are published by Bantam Books, a division of Bantam Doubleday Dell Publishing Group, Inc. Its trademark, consisting of the words "Bantam Books" and the portrayal of a rooster, is Registered in U.S. Patent and Trademark Office and in other countries. Marca Registrada. Bantam Books, 666 Fifth Avenue, New York, New York 10103.

Printed and bound in Great Britain by
Cox & Wyman Ltd., Reading

Crossed Signals

Chapter One

"C'mon, Amy. It'll be *fun!*" It didn't seem possible, but Laura Newman's big eyes grew even wider as she pleaded with her best friend.

"Sure, about as much fun as Suzanne had on that date you set up for her last summer." Amy knew she was a pushover when it came to her best friend, Laura, but she told herself to be strong this time. She really didn't want to go on a blind date Saturday night.

"Be fair." Laura smoothed her short dark hair behind her ears. "I didn't know the guy was going to be so boring that she'd fall asleep in her pizza at Torelli's."

"It took her a week to get all the cheese out of her hair!" Amy chuckled, then quickly resumed a stern expression. She was exaggerating, but she had to make her point. Blind dates were always disastrous.

"But this will be a double date—blind date," Laura said brightly. "If Tommy Carter turns out to be a loser, I'll be there to keep you awake." Laura rubbed her hands together. "Besides, I don't think there'll be any danger of you getting bored. Ben Richardson has four tickets to the Yellow Dog concert."

"Bow wow." Amy grimaced. Laura loved heavy metal, and Ronnie Smithson, the lead singer in Yellow Dog, was her favorite rock star. Unfortunately Amy hated heavy metal.

"Did I make fun of Bruce when you made me stand in line with you overnight for Springsteen tickets?" Laura reminded her.

Laura wasn't playing fair. "I didn't exactly twist your arm," said Amy. "I remember you begging to come with me when you heard that a certain guy had already taken his sleeping bag to the auditorium for the camp-out."

"But then I found out he'd brought his girlfriend along with him, and all I got was cold feet," Laura complained.

Amy could see she wasn't going to get very far trying to be logical with her friend. Maybe the direct approach would work better. "Look, Laura. I'd rather just stay home Saturday night."

"On the last weekend of our Christmas vacation? Are you crazy?" Laura pushed Amy down on the couch. "I don't think you're feeling quite right."

Amy sat up straight and hugged one of the pillows Mrs. Newman had needlepointed. "There's nothing wrong with a person not getting excited about a blind date."

"Okay." Laura started pacing the length of her living room. "Forget the blind date part. Think about the concert."

"But I hate heavy metal," Amy reminded her friend.

"I think your brain is getting soft from listening to too much top-ten junk on the radio. Can you honestly say Ronnie Smithson doesn't make you drool?" Laura pressed a hand dramatically to her heart.

"The blond party *animal* they named the band after?" Amy had seen him in videos, parading across the stage with his long blond hair flying behind him. She wasn't impressed.

"Mmmm," Laura agreed, not catching Amy's sarcasm. "Just think what a good view we'll have from the third row!"

Laura squeezed her eyes shut, lost in the sheer pleasure of imagining herself that close to the stage and Ronnie Smithson, while Amy wondered where her mother kept the earplugs. She knew her best friend would do anything to see Yellow Dog. There was no way she was going to get out of this date short of moving to China.

"Tell me about the guys," Amy asked, resigned to her fate.

"The guys? You mean you'll do it?" Laura grabbed Amy in a bear hug that pulled her to her feet.

"Yeah. I'll do it . . . unless my date is some kind of mutant."

"The guys aren't bad," Laura said, heading into the kitchen. She got two colas out of the refrigerator and casually flipped the tops open.

"You said my guy's Tommy Carter?" Amy asked, pouring her soda into a glass. "Who's he?"

Laura brought the cookie jar to the kitchen table. "He's on the ski team."

"Not the guy with long dark hair that hangs over his collar?" She'd seen him leaving for practice with his hair sticking out from under his ski hat.

"It's not that long," Laura said, pulling a home-baked chocolate-chip cookie out of the jar. "I think he's kind of cute."

"He's okay," Amy allowed. "What about your date, Ben Richardson?"

"He just moved here in October from Chicago. His dad was transferred."

"Then how did he get Yellow Dog tickets?" Amy asked. "I thought they'd been sold out for months." Was there a slim chance the date might not happen?

"I heard he got them from people at work or something like that." Laura flicked her hand as if to say it didn't matter to her where he'd gotten his third-row tickets.

"Is he cute?" Amy wanted to know, finding a cookie for herself.

"If you like his type," Laura said mysteriously.

"What type?"

"He seems pretty ambitious. In a few months, he's gotten to know most of the right people."

"And you're not interested in him?" He sounded like someone Laura should be dying to know.

"A lot of girls think he's cute," Laura said, wrinkling her nose. "But he's got curly hair."

Amy laughed. It was a well-known fact that Laura loved guys, but she thought curly hair was a fatal flaw. "If a lot of girls think he's cute, then why does he need a blind date for the concert?"

"He and I don't have a blind date," Laura explained. "He's seen me."

"Don't get technical," Amy said. "I'm just asking why a popular guy doesn't have three friends he'd like to take to the concert."

"He probably does." Laura grinned wickedly. "I heard about his tickets last night and was on his doorstep at nine o'clock this morning to work out a deal with him."

"Laura! You'd do anything to go to this concert, wouldn't you?" Amy shook her head.

"I'm not so different from you," Laura claimed. "I'd do anything for Yellow Dog, and you'd do anything for a friend."

"What happened to you?" Laura cried on Saturday evening when Amy arrived for their double date. She covered her face with her hands.

"I'll tell you if you'll let me in." Amy scrunched her shoulders nearly to her ears, trying to protect herself from the icy January wind. Standing on the Newmans' doorstep while Laura had hysterics wasn't her idea of fun. "I'm freezing out here."

Laura stepped back from the door to let Amy into her house. After Amy unwrapped the scarf from her neck, Laura leaned close to get a better look at Amy's face.

"It's a black eye," Amy explained.

"I can see that," Laura said with a sigh. "But how did it get there?"

"I was playing racquetball with my dad this afternoon—"

"—and you got hit with the ball?" Laura frowned. "I told you racquetball was too dangerous."

"It was an accident," Amy insisted. "I'm just learning to play and I'm not very good at it."

"Obviously." Laura sighed. "But how could you *do* something like this right before the concert?"

Lights shone in the driveway, and Laura quickly reached for her trendy leather jacket. "They're here!"

Amy felt a twinge of annoyance; it seemed as if Laura's only concern was for her stupid concert. Laura was already in the car by the time Amy took a deep breath and told herself to try, at least, to have a good time.

She slid into the backseat and smiled at her date. "Hi, I'm Amy."

"Hi, Amy. I'm Tommy." He blinked and took a second look at her. "You have a black eye."

"Yeah." *Give him two points for being observant,* Amy thought. Laura's date turned around from the front seat to look at her.

"Are you sure you're okay?"

Amy saw concern in his friendly brown eyes. "I'm all right. It's just a little bruise."

He offered her a crooked grin, and Amy's breath caught in her throat. Maybe Laura didn't think he was cute, but Amy thought he was adorable with his wavy reddish brown hair and warm amber eyes, and she liked the little space between his front teeth when he grinned.

"We haven't been introduced. I'm Ben Richardson." He reached his right arm over the seat to shake hands.

She put her mittened hand inside his bare one. "I'm Amy Tyler."

"Can we get going?" Laura asked impatiently from the front seat. "I'd hate to miss a minute of the concert."

Ben took his hand back and put the car in gear. "No problem." As soon as they were on the road, he glanced into his rearview mirror and found Amy. "How did you get the shiner?"

"Racquetball."

"You play?"

"Not very well. I'm just learning."

"You should wear goggles." Amy was going to say something about how ugly they were until he added, "I do."

"I'll remember that," she said instead.

"I got a black eye last winter when someone's

ski pole hit me in the face on the team bus," Tommy volunteered.

"They're pretty terrible, aren't they?" Ben said. "I got one last summer playing baseball. First they hurt, then they turn all kinds of colors."

"You play baseball?" Laura inquired. "Are you going out for Madison's team in the spring?"

"I don't know. Transferring in your senior year is pretty hard. I'm sure the team has plenty of good players already."

"They took first place in the conference last year," Laura said proudly. Amy remembered her friend had been dating one of the pitchers for a few weeks during the season.

"See? They won't need me," Ben concluded. "What do you do when you're not going to concerts?" he asked Laura.

"School keeps me busy," Laura said vaguely. Amy stifled a laugh. For the past year and a half her friend had dedicated herself to dating. She changed boyfriends more often than some girls changed their earrings, and that took a lot of time and energy. But it was hardly something she could tell Ben.

"What about you, Amy?" he asked next.

"Me?" She didn't expect him to include her in his conversation, but she appreciated it.

"Besides playing racquetball," he teased.

"I spend a lot of time with my friends and homework takes forever some nights. Then I do some volunteer stuff." Laura groaned, and Amy got the message. What guy would be interested in hearing about her volunteer work at the Golden Oaks nursing home?

"What about you?" Laura asked Ben.

"Besides school and trying to make new friends, I have to keep this thing running." He tapped the steering wheel.

Amy could tell it was an older car, but she wasn't good at recognizing models. "What kind is it?"

"A 1980 Camaro," he said proudly. "Over vacation I put in a new sound system. I work at WMXX part-time to support my habit."

"The TV station?" Laura sounded very interested. "What do you do there?"

"Run errands and help wherever they need me."

"That's nice . . ." Laura's disappointment was obvious to Amy. Although her date worked in a glamorous place, his job sounded too ordinary for Laura.

"I like it," he said. "They gave me the tickets for tonight."

"You got the Yellow Dog tickets from the people you work with?" Laura asked in disbelief.

He had finally earned her interest. "Do you think they might have a job for me?"

Ben glanced over at Laura, and Amy thought she caught a small smile on his lips when he asked, "Do you type?"

Luckily they were turning in to the auditorium parking lot and Laura let the subject drop. She was the first one out of the car, and she started toward the auditorium without even bothering to wait for her date.

"We're going to miss the first song," she warned the others.

Ben hurried to catch up with Laura while Amy waited for Tommy to help her out of the backseat. He opened the door and just stood there. Amy had expected him to offer a hand. When he didn't, she slowly climbed out of the car. She wasn't exactly in a hurry.

The guys weren't bad, she mused; she was just dreading subjecting her eardrums to Yellow Dog. Tommy seemed nice enough—but he was awfully quiet. Maybe he'd spent a little too much time alone on the slopes with only the snow for company. But Laura's date was something else. Amy liked Ben's warm, friendly manner. She couldn't understand why Laura wasn't more interested in him.

Moments before the lights dimmed, the girls

and their dates slid into their third-row seats. Laura took the seat on the aisle. Ben was next to her, leaving Amy between the guys. The lights dimmed, and Laura started to scream. Amy put her hands over her ears. Laura was already screaming. When the spotlight zeroed in on Ronnie Smithson as he jumped off a platform to center stage, Laura went wild, along with thousands of other Yellow Dog fans.

"You know I want ya baby," he screeched, before the screaming crowd drowned out the next line of his song. On the chorus, colored spotlights revealed the rest of the band. In a moment Laura was on her feet, jumping and clapping her hands.

Ben leaned close to Amy, putting his mouth next to her ear. "Isn't this great?"

She turned to look at him, nearly bumping his nose with hers. She agreed with little enthusiasm. "Yeah. Great."

"You don't sound convinced."

She read his lips more than heard his comment. Taking a deep breath, she screamed back, "He's not my favorite singer."

Ben nodded as though he felt the same way. He cupped his hands over his mouth and started to speak, and Amy moved closer so he could press his hands to her ear. "Forget Smithson, he's a jerk. But listen to Will Franklin on the bass. He's the best in the world."

Amy nodded and tried to concentrate on the rhythms coming from Franklin's guitar instead of Ronnie Smithson's stage antics. Ben was right. The guy could do amazing things with his guitar. She'd never noticed that before, although she had listened to Laura's tapes more times than she cared to remember.

When Will Franklin stepped forward to do a solo, Amy found herself grinning. Ben nudged her with his elbow. "What do you think?"

"He's great!"

"You're having fun?" he shouted.

For a second Amy wondered why Ben was asking her the question instead of his own date, but then she noticed Laura standing on her chair clapping her hands high over her head. It was obvious her friend was having a wonderful time.

The amazing thing was that Amy was enjoying the concert, too. "Yeah. I'm glad I came," she admitted.

Chapter Two

Amy was writing a letter at the kitchen table late the next morning when someone pounded at the back door. Since her parents had met some friends for brunch, Amy peeked through the curtain to see who was knocking so hard. When she recognized Laura under the red ski cap, she waved.

Laura stepped into the house and stomped the snow off her boots on the rug by the door. She didn't say anything as she yanked off her boots and walked into the kitchen in her stockinged feet. Then she hung her jacket and cap over a chair and rubbed her arms, trying to warm them.

"You look cold," Amy finally said.

"What's that supposed to mean?" snapped Laura unexpectedly.

"Your face is all red. You must have taken a long walk before you came over here." Amy explained, a little confused by her friend's tone of voice.

"I was thinking," Laura said mysteriously.

"About the concert?" Amy asked, thinking Laura must have been walking around daydreaming about Ronnie Smithson.

Laura stared at Amy. "Yeah, the concert—we've got to talk. Where are your parents?"

"At the Chalet, having brunch with friends."

"But they could come home soon." Laura started out of the kitchen. "Let's talk in your room."

Amy followed her friend up the stairs, confused by Laura's mood. She sounded upset, but what about the concert could have bothered her? It had seemed like she'd had a terrific time. Unless she'd had some secret dream about meeting the band and was disappointed it hadn't happened.

Laura sat on the bed, so Amy turned on the radio and settled into the maple rocking chair by the window. Whatever was bothering Laura, it was clear she wanted to talk it out.

"What do you have to say for yourself?" Laura asked finally.

"Me?" Amy thought *Laura* was the one with the problem. What was she supposed to say? "You were right, a blind date wasn't so bad. I had a good time last night."

"A good time," Laura snorted.

"I know I made a big deal about hating Yellow Dog, but it was different being there in person, I guess." The evening had certainly turned out so much better than she'd expected.

"Being there in person? Or being there with *Ben?*" Laura inquired.

"Ben was your date," Amy said, confused.

"I'm glad you noticed." Laura frowned. "He sure spent enough time talking to *you.*"

"He was pointing out some things about the band," Amy said in all honesty. "Besides, you were too busy screaming for Ronnie to make much conversation."

"And what about him insisting you choose the place to eat after the concert?" Laura asked, ignoring her friend's point.

"You seemed too tired to have an opinion, and I don't think Tommy Carter could care less where he eats—as long as they have cheeseburgers." Amy started to rock gently in her chair.

She wasn't exactly sure what Laura was getting at, but the conversation was making her uncomfortable.

"I wasn't too tired to talk at the restaurant, but Ben didn't seem interested in talking to me," Laura said with a pout.

"I guess he and I did monopolize the conversation," Amy admitted. It had been so easy talking with him. He was a fun guy.

"That's it?" Laura raised her eyebrows. "Aren't you sorry?"

"Sorry?" Amy couldn't think of a single reason to be sorry. First Laura had begged her to enjoy the double date, and now that she had—

"He was *my* date," Laura said bluntly.

Amy was dumbfounded. "And you're mad because he *talked* to me?"

"Talked to you . . . fussed over you . . ." Laura shook her head as though the list of offenses were so long she couldn't finish naming them all.

When Laura put it that way, Amy could see that Ben might have paid a little too much attention to her. "But you said you didn't even like him. You said he wasn't your type. And you said you went out with him just because he had the tickets."

Amy was tempted to say something mean like reminding Laura how little attention she had paid to Ben Richardson, *her date*, last night. But Laura was her good friend, and Amy wanted to understand what was behind her mood and patch things up between them.

"Did you suddenly decide you like Ben or something?"

Laura picked up Amy's old stuffed bear and tugged on his ears. "He's all right . . . but I don't really want to go out with him again."

"Then why are you so upset? I wasn't trying to steal him from you. And even if I had been trying, you don't want him," Amy said very logically.

"But it was so embarrassing!" Laura finally confessed.

"Why? We didn't see anyone we knew at the concert." Everyone at the concert had seemed so wrapped up in the music that Amy didn't think anyone would have noticed if Ben had stood on his head.

"No one else had to see it," Laura insisted. "I knew what was happening, and I was mortified."

At last Amy understood. In her typically dramatic fashion, Laura's pride had been hurt. She was proud of the impression she made on guys. To be overlooked by a date, even a date she didn't care about, would be humiliating for Laura Newman.

"I'm sorry." Now that she knew where her friend was coming from, Amy could apologize sincerely. She had never meant to hurt Laura's feelings.

"What are you going to do if he calls and asks you out?" Laura asked suddenly.

"He won't."

"How can you be sure? He seemed to like you." Laura sounded worried.

"If he did call—which he won't—what would it matter?" Amy wasn't letting herself think Ben might call. There was no chance of that happening. He had just wanted someone to talk to last night.

"It would matter because I told a lot of people I was going to the concert with him. If you were to show up with him next week, people would wonder why he dumped me."

Amy nodded slowly. Laura's reason made sense, but Amy couldn't quite see that it was important enough for them to be arguing about it. "Look, this is silly. Ben's a senior and we're juniors. James Madison is a big school. What are the odds I'll even talk to him again?"

"I suppose you're right," Laura said slowly.

"So we can forget about Ben Richardson?" Amy hoped the subject was closed.

"All right. We've got more important things to talk about anyway." Laura's dark eyes twinkled, and she scooted to the edge of the bed. "Suzanne's birthday is two weeks from yesterday."

"Do you want to have a party for her?"

"What do you think about a slumber party . . . a *surprise* slumber party?"

Amy smiled. It was Laura's style to want to make the party a surprise. She got out of the rocking chair and rummaged in her desk drawer for a sheet of paper. "Sounds good, let's start planning it."

They made up the guest list and talked about the kinds of food they needed. Laura volunteered to call KWAK and arrange for the night disc jockey to mention Suzanne during the party. Amy's job was to talk her mother into letting them have the party in the Tylers' downstairs family room. By the time Laura left, neither girl was thinking about Ben Richardson.

Amy's lasagna lunch was sitting in her stomach like a lump of lead when she walked upstairs to her first American history class of the semester the following Monday afternoon. It amazed her that she could get decent grades in math and impress Ms. Hampton with her English papers, but she was an absolute disaster with memorizing dates and all the other things that seemed so important in history. It didn't help that her father studied history as a hobby and more than anything wanted to share his interest with her.

Feeling sorry for herself, Amy slid into a desk in the back row without looking around her. She opened her notebook to write down the assignment, which would probably be a hundred pages of reading due tomorrow.

"Hi, Amy! I didn't know I'd be in your history class."

She looked up, wondering who could be so cheerful about spending the next hour with George Washington or Ethan What's-his-name or Andrew Jackson. "Ben!"

He offered her a crooked grin just as he had Saturday night, and Amy wondered if he always smiled that way. "You look pretty good today."

Her mouth fell open at the unexpected compliment.

"I meant your eye," he said awkwardly. He pointed to her face. "It's not puffy or anything."

Actually the skin under her eye had been mauve with a hint of green that morning before she spent twenty minutes with concealer and makeup. But she wasn't going to reveal her beauty secret. Instead she said, "It feels much better."

"That's good." He stood with his hands at his sides, apparently waiting for her to say something.

"Are you in this class?"

He checked his class schedule. "This *is* American history, isn't it?"

"Yes it is," Amy answered, puzzled. American history was a junior class. "I thought you were a senior."

He rolled his eyes. "I am, but in my old school American history was a senior class. I took world history last year."

"And that's what the seniors are taking this year at Madison." Now she understood why he'd come over to talk to her. He probably didn't know many juniors in the class.

"Is this seat taken?" he asked, pointing to the desk next to her.

Amy thought about Laura, then pushed the thought aside. It wasn't as though she were planning to make a move on Ben during Mr. Wilson's first lecture. Ben Richardson was still a new kid in school, and Amy just wanted to help him out. Besides, Laura wouldn't deny Amy a chance to have a little fun in a class that usually gave her nightmares. Seeing a friendly face had made her feel better already.

"Sit down," she said, after considering all the factors.

"Thanks." He dropped his notebook on the desktop as he sat down and stretched his legs out under the desk. "Can you hear yet? Or are your ears still ringing from Saturday night?"

Pretending she had been deafened by Yellow Dog's music, she put her left hand to her ear. "Pardon me?"

He threw back his head and laughed just as the teacher walked into the room. "I'm glad to see people are happy to be here," Mr. Wilson said from the front of the room.

"Real happy," Amy muttered under her breath.

Ben glanced in her direction, but he didn't have a chance to say anything because the class bell rang. Amy doodled for most of the hour while the teacher described how much material they would cover during the quarter and then told them how much fun they were going to have doing the work. He seemed determined to have a happy class.

Mr. Wilson lifted the heavy textbook. "At the

end of last quarter, my class was up to the firing on Fort Sumter. But I see a lot of new faces out there. Help me see how much you know."

Amy heard the words as the introduction to a pop quiz, or something teachers liked to call a pretest. Whatever they called it, it was one more chance for her to show how little she could remember. To her surprise, the teacher started asking the class questions.

"What was the Missouri Compromise?"

Ben raised his hand, but the teacher called on a girl in the front of the class. "When Missouri joined the Union," she said, "some representatives wanted to prohibit slavery in the new state. Finally it was admitted as a slave state, but all states north of Missouri joining after that had to be free states."

"Thirty-six, thirty," Ben mumbled to himself.

Amy was impressed when the teacher clarified that the boundary in question was thirty six degrees, thirty minutes north latitude. She vaguely remembered the terms from eighth-grade geography, but Ben had known the exact place Mr. Wilson had had in mind.

The teacher continued asking questions until he had the class talking about the various debates and other compromises related to the issue of slavery. Ben had finally gotten his chance to speak when he'd described the Dred Scott decision. "It was the U.S. Supreme Court's conclusion that Congress could not prohibit slavery in the territories and that they were, in fact, bound to protect it," he'd explained. Amy was impressed again by his knowledge.

Ten minutes before the hour ended, Mr. Wilson tried to sum up the discussion. "We've been reviewing the things that were happening in the country before Lincoln's inauguration. Has it given you a good feel for the tinderbox the country was when the Confederates fired on Fort Sumter?"

For the first time, isolated dates and names started coming together for Amy. Instead of worrying about the little pieces, Mr. Wilson was showing her the whole picture. Just when she almost felt encouraged, he said, "For those of you who don't quite remember the details, a quick review of chapters eighteen and nineteen would be useful."

This class wasn't going to be any different from all the other history classes in her past, Amy thought with a sigh. Although Mr. Wilson could make it sound a little more interesting, he still wanted them to learn all the dates, names, and places.

"The textbook covers the Civil War pretty well," Mr. Wilson continued, "but it doesn't give us a *real* picture of the times. It's going to be up to you to fill out that picture."

Wonderful. More reading. Amy could see herself never leaving the house for the next three weeks while she tried to muddle through more books on the Civil War.

"It will be more interesting if you work with partners. There are a lot of things you can do to find out more about the Civil War. You can read old diaries, make a series of maps to show the battles, or . . . " He passed out a two-page list showing the kinds of projects his students had done in the past. "Of course, we'll all want to know what each group discovers, so each pair will do an oral presentation."

An oral presentation? The assignment boggled her mind. Was he going to make her embarrass herself in front of the whole class?

The bell rang, and Ben leaned toward Amy. "Wanna be my partner?"

Her head was spinning. What had she done to deserve such a lucky break? Ben seemed to know all the answers in class. He could be the solution to all her problems.

"Don't you want to work with me?" he asked when she was speechless.

She reached out for his arm before he could misunderstand her silence. The grade they could get on the joint project could be the difference between her usual C minus and a C plus in the class. "I'd really like to work with you."

He looked surprised as her fingertips brushed his sleeve, but he didn't say anything to make her feel self-conscious. He just grinned, and the smile reflected in his amber eyes. "Great, let's get together one afternoon this week."

Chapter Three

"Your house is great!" Amy told Ben the next afternoon.

"My mom's been decorating it," he said as if all the trendy furniture and artwork didn't impress him.

"She's good." The house was the exact opposite of the comfortable, country decor in Amy's house. Although she loved living in her home, there was something exciting about the high ceiling, white walls, and the peach sectional in Ben's living room.

"She has to be good. It's her job," he explained. "She had her own business back in Chicago, and she's working hard to get customers here." He slipped out of his lined leather jacket and helped Amy take off her parka. Ben tossed them both on a chrome coatrack and asked, "Are you hungry?"

"Thirsty." Amy didn't feel comfortable raiding Mrs. Richardson's cupboards. She followed Ben into the kitchen. He took her books and dumped everything on the breakfast counter while she stood in awe in the doorway. Until now, she'd only seen a sophisticated, gourmet kitchen like this in magazines. "Your mom must cook a lot, too."

Ben opened the refrigerator door and stuck his head inside. His answer was muffled. "No. Cooking is my dad's hobby."

He backed out of the refrigerator juggling a loaf of bread, a jar of mayonnaise, a package of cold cuts, and two liter bottles of soda. After carefully setting the bottles on the snack bar, he let the bread drop out of his arms. "Diet or the regular stuff?" he asked.

Boys seemed to expect girls to drink diet soda but Amy hated the taste of artificial sweeteners. "The real stuff, please," she said.

He smiled. "Me, too. Could you get the glasses?" Ben nodded toward the cabinet next to the sink. "They're up there."

Amy poured drinks for both of them while Ben made a sandwich. She wondered at how comfortable she felt. It was Ben, she thought for a moment, then she shook off the feeling. She was here to work on a history project, that was *all*.

With his sandwich ready, Ben pulled two stools up to the counter and motioned for Amy to sit. Between bites he said, "I talked to Mr. Wilson about an idea I had for our project."

"You did?" Amy had read the list five times, trying to find a project that looked easy. It wasn't that she didn't want to work hard, but history wasn't exactly her forte.

He looked over at her, slight uncertainty in his eyes. "I hope you don't mind . . ."

"Well, what did you pick?" she asked.

"The Battle of Bull Run."

He took another bite of his sandwich while Amy stared at him, waiting for more information. What did he plan to do with Bull Run? It sounded more boring than hard.

"What about Bull Run?" she asked.

"It was the battle that everyone thought the Union soldiers could win with their eyes closed. People actually came to watch, the same way we get together to watch a football game. The Union was totally whipped."

"So what are we going to do? Read a hundred stories about the battle?" She couldn't help wrinkling her nose as she took a sip of her drink. His enthusiasm was not contagious.

"No, we're going to be General McDowell and General Beauregard."

Amy choked on her soda. "What?"

"I thought it would be fun if we pretended to be the two generals offering our separate views about the battle . . . how we prepared, what happened, and what we thought might happen afterward. It would be like the generals were being interviewed right after the battle."

Amy had to admit it sounded more interesting than reading aloud a book report, but it would take a lot of work to get ready for their presentation. "How do we find out all the things we need to know?"

"I've been checking into that." Ben unzipped his backpack and pulled out a thick library book. He took a minute to find the bibliography buried in the last pages. "This lists lots of sources."

Amy groaned. There had to be two hundred books in the bibliography. "We're going to read all of these?"

"No," he said laughing. "We wouldn't be able to *find* half of the books. Most of them are old out-of-print things published over fifty years ago."

He pointed out a half dozen books that they should try to find at the library. One of the titles looked familiar. "I think my dad has this book," Amy cried in surprise.

"He does?" Ben sounded happy. "That's the one Mr. Wilson said we should be sure to find."

"Does that mean I have to read the whole thing? It's thousands of pages long." Amy hoped she didn't sound lazy, but she couldn't imagine plodding all the way through the thick book with microscopic print.

"I could look at it and see how much each of us needs to actually study," Ben suggested.

"Okay," Amy said. It might be kind of fun learning about her character once she knew what things to read. "I'll bring the book to school tomorrow."

"If it's not too heavy," he teased.

"I'm strong." Amy flexed her left arm, her muscles hidden under her Esprit sweatshirt.

"I'll take your word for it." Ben made himself a second sandwich with the excuse, "My parents are coming home late tonight."

"Your family sounds a lot like mine." The similarities surprised Amy, considering how different their homes were.

"Your mom spends a lot of time hanging out at other people's houses?" Ben inquired.

Amy laughed, trying to imagine her mother as a trendy interior designer. "My mom teaches second grade at Grove Elementary."

"But I thought you said she wasn't home much." Ben reached for the cookie jar and offered Amy a homemade gingersnap.

"She's involved with a lot of parent-teacher deals and a youth counseling program and she's always taking some class at night."

"Wow! And your dad?"

"He's a vice president at the First Western Bank."

Ben whistled. "It never hurts to have a few connections at the bank."

"It's not like they let him bring the money home for the weekend," she said, using a joke her friends all liked.

He threw his head back and laughed just as he had done yesterday in history. Listening to him, Amy got tingles down to her toes.

"My mom is busy trying to get clients in town," Ben told Amy when he caught his breath again. "She talks to any group that will invite her, she goes to seminars just so she can hand her business cards to the people she meets . . ."

"It sounds like moving was very hard for her," Amy said sympathetically.

"It was hard for all of us." Ben's voice suddenly went soft. "My dad says he's still trying to figure out the power politics at corporate headquarters. He used to be a regional manager for U.S. Electronics, but the big office here is a whole new world."

Amy sucked in her breath when she heard Ben's dad was a big shot at U.S. Electronics, one of the most important companies in the state. No wonder he lived in one of the most exclusive neighborhoods.

Ben didn't notice her silence as he continued. "My mom had fifty important clients back in Chicago. She decorated office buildings and mansions. She barely knows anyone here."

He rubbed his chin, and Amy could tell there was more on his mind. He'd been talking about how the move had affected his parents. She wondered how he felt about it. "What about you, Ben?"

"Me?" He swallowed twice before he tried to express his thoughts. "My life was just the way I wanted it to be back there. I had a lot of friends. I played on the baseball team that went to the state finals last year." Ben placed his right elbow on the counter and rested his chin in his palm. "Would you believe I was elected senior class president two weeks before my dad found out he was being transferred?"

Amy wanted, really wanted, to put her arm around his shoulders. Coming to Madison High in October, there was no way he could have the year he'd left behind in Chicago. All she could say was, "That's so sad."

He sighed heavily. "I try not to think about it too much. I just have to make the best of what I've found here."

Amy admired his strength. She couldn't imagine giving up her friends or life at Madison High, not to mention the house she'd lived in all of her life. "What have you liked about Madison so far?"

"It's kinda hard getting into a group when most of the people have known each other for years, but everyone has been friendly and helpful."

"That's good. But have you gotten involved in anything?"

"Not really," he admitted. "I've been talking to someone at the university, and they advised me to get serious about my grades this year if I want to get into the journalism program."

"Journalism?" Amy didn't know many people who had given much serious thought to a career. "That's ambitious."

"Don't you have plans?" he asked.

"I've thought of being a teacher like my mom, but I'm not sure yet."

"I've known for three years that I want to be a newsman," Ben told her.

"Like the ten o'clock anchorman on channel WMXX?" she teased.

"Don't laugh. You never know." He walked to the sink to rinse off his plate. "I mean, I'm already working there part-time."

"That's right!" He had mentioned that on the way to the concert. "What do you actually do there?"

"Everything that no one else wants to do," he said. "When the office staff runs out of coffee, I drive to the grocery store before anyone has a caffeine attack. Last week a photographer's car overheated at an accident scene. I had to pick up his film and rush it back to the studio so the story could be on the six o'clock news."

"That's really exciting," Amy said as they walked into the family room beyond the kitchen.

"Don't sit on the furniture," he warned her. "It's like sitting on a stack of bricks." He grabbed some oversize pillows from behind a chair and tossed them on the floor. She sat on one, and he pulled another close to hers. "The job isn't that exciting. After they threw confetti around for someone's birthday, I got to sweep up the floor. They didn't even save me a piece of cake," he grumbled in mock disgust.

"But it must be great being in a real TV studio." If a person had to sweep floors, sweeping a television studio was more interesting than cleaning up her mother's classroom after the second graders had trashed it.

"Sometimes I get to do fun things," he confessed. "Like tomorrow afternoon. I get to pick up Elle Rico at her hotel and take her to the studio for an interview. The driver they usually use had another job."

"Elle Rico!" Amy screamed. She was only the best actress on "Another Day," the soap opera Amy and all her friends watched whenever they were home sick or on vacation.

"You know her?"

"Not personally," Amy said quickly. "I just love the part she plays on 'Another Day.' "

"Yeah?" It was obvious he was not a fan. "They showed me her picture yesterday, and she is beautiful." Amy nodded in agreement. Without any warning, Ben asked, "Would you like to go out with me Friday night?"

Amy gulped. "Go out with you?" she repeated, a trifle too shrilly.

"They're doing *South Pacific* at the Playhouse,"

he said, kindly ignoring her surprise. "Do you like musicals?"

That was a question she could answer without thinking for a second. "I love them. In fact, Madison High put on *South Pacific* just last spring."

"Were you in it?"

"Hardly," Amy giggled. "They didn't even let me try out."

"At my old school anyone could try out if they wanted to," Ben said, unable to keep the pride out of his voice. It was clear he still loved his old school.

"They didn't exactly keep me away from the auditions." Amy couldn't believe she was about to share her most humbling experience with him. "When I got up on the stage I sang one line and then my mind went blank. There was no way I was ever going to remember the rest of the song, but I offered to try again. Do you know what they told me?"

He shook his head, looking anxious to hear what had happened to her.

"They told me not to bother . . . they didn't need to hear any more! Can you think of a better way for them to say they didn't want me in the show?"

Ben covered his mouth to hide his smile.

Amy liked the idea that he was too nice to burst into laughter over her disaster. Finally he said soberly, "I guess you couldn't mistake their meaning."

"Now I just sing in the shower," she confessed.

"Was this experience so embarrassing that you'd rather die than see *South Pacific* again?" he asked.

He wanted to know if she would go to the play with him. What was she supposed to say? When Laura had worried what would happen if Ben asked Amy out, they'd resolved the matter by agreeing she'd probably never see him again. Well, she'd seen him. And now he was asking her out. What was she supposed to do?

"Look, Amy," he said when she was quiet too long. "If the play makes you uncomfortable, we could do something else."

Amy was touched by his concern. "The audition wasn't terminal," she informed him. "I'm just not sure about my plans for Friday night."

"You already have a date," he concluded, looking disappointed.

"No." She wouldn't lie about having a boyfriend. "But there could be some family plans . . ."

"Could you tell me tomorrow?"

"Sure," she said with more confidence than she felt.

"Why don't I stop by your house after work tomorrow?" he asked. "I can pick up that history book, and you can check the calendar at home."

"Okay." He couldn't know how much she appreciated his attitude. Instead of pressuring her, he was making things easy for her.

"Now, back to the history project," said Amy, anxious to change the subject. "I feel kind of guilty that you're doing all the heavy reading. What can I do until you've found the stuff I need to read for my role? Or don't you want to do the McDowell-Beauregard routine now that you know I'm such a horrible actress?"

"I thought it was just your singing that was bad."

She blushed.

"Why don't you find out what our class history book says about the Battle of Bull Run and decide which general you want to be?"

"Okay." Now she had to review last quarter's chapters to get ready for Mr. Wilson's next class and read ahead in the book to be prepared for her next meeting with Ben. Whether she liked it or not, she was going to be working hard in history this quarter.

A grandfather clock clanged somewhere in the house, and Amy checked her watch. "Six o'clock! I was supposed to be home half an hour ago . . . starting dinner."

Ben jumped to his feet. "I'll drive you home."

He pulled his keys out of his jeans pocket while Amy wrapped up in her down parka and cap. He popped a Yellow Dog tape into his cassette player as they drove the five miles to her house.

"I promise not to bug you at school tomorrow about the play," he said as she got out of the car. "But tell me you'll think about it."

"I will," she said, waving as she backed down the driveway. There was no doubt she would spend more time worrying about the invitation tonight than reading history.

Chapter Four

"That pink sweater—the one you wanted for Christmas, but didn't get—is on sale at Dayton's," Suzanne told Laura after school on Wednesday.

Laura tried to sip her hot chocolate, but it was too hot, and she set it down on the table quickly. Normally they came to the Tiger's Den for sodas during the afternoon, but the weather had turned nasty.

"That sweater was great. I sure could have used it today," Laura said. "How much is it?"

"Marked down fifteen percent!"

Amy let them plan their shopping expedition without any input from her. True to his word, Ben hadn't mentioned the date during history class, but he would be stopping by her house when he finished working at WMXX. She still didn't know what she was going to tell him.

Amy did know one thing for sure; she really wanted to go to the play with him Friday night. The morning-after-the-concert scene with Laura had played through her mind continuously since Ben had left her on her doorstep yesterday. The question she couldn't answer was how Laura really felt about Ben.

Her friend had claimed she'd set up the double date just to get tickets to the Yellow Dog concert. In fact, Laura's usual enthusiasm about the guys she dated had been conspicuously missing when she first told Amy about the plan, and again during the actual date. If she liked Ben, she'd been hiding it very well. But Amy had seen her best friend play it cool with guys before. Any knew her decision hinged on one thing: how serious had Laura been when she said her problem Sunday morning was nothing more than wounded pride?

"Oh no!" Laura grabbed a menu and hid behind it.

"What *now*?" Suzanne inquired, pushing her long blond hair over her shoulders. Amy had to laugh. Suzanne liked Laura a lot, but she didn't have much patience for her dramatics.

"Up at the cash register . . . just leaving. It's

my un-date, Ben Richardson," Laura whispered as if there were some danger he might hear her over the dull roar of twenty different conversations.

Amy swallowed hard and wished she could hide behind a menu, too, but that would make her friends curious. Under the table, she crossed her fingers and hoped with all her heart Ben hadn't seen her. Fortunately he hadn't. He waved to some guys at the back of the restaurant and hurried out the door. Amy remembered he had to pick up the soap opera star and take her to the studio today.

"I still don't know why you're so bitter," Suzanne was saying. "I mean, you guys had a business deal about the tickets. He wasn't interested in you and you weren't interested in him. Now you're upset because he didn't fall all over you. Does that make any sense?"

"I guess you had to be there," Laura mumbled. "Right, *Amy*?"

Amy's heart was beating furiously as she glanced down at the table. She didn't want to talk about Ben Richardson.

"He hasn't called you, has he?" Suzanne asked.

Amy cleared her throat to keep from squeaking. "Called? No." It wasn't a lie, she told herself. He had not telephoned her.

"Maybe he is a jerk," Suzanne told Laura. "After coming on to Amy the way he did at the concert, you'd think he would have called."

Amy's palms were clammy and her head was spinning as she willed herself to stay quiet. What could she say anyway? They were partners on a history project. She had agreed to that, at least in the beginning, because it would give her a chance to raise her grade—and what could she say about the date now, after letting them think she hadn't heard from him? She couldn't ask them for advice. Amy would have to decide on her own whether or not to see *South Pacific* with Ben.

"Oooh!" Laura fussed with her already perfect hair as she glanced up at the doorway. "Do you guys know Scott Dunnel?"

"Only the most popular, most eligible guy in the senior class," Suzanne chanted, repeating Laura's usual description of the boy.

"He just walked in with a bunch of friends." Laura always used hushed tones when she talked about the perfect Scott Dunnel.

The boys found a table not far from Laura, Suzanne, and Amy. After they got settled, a blond boy kept looking over at them.

"The guy in the red sweater is watching you," Suzanne informed Laura.

"Mike Norton," Laura said quickly. She turned and smiled at him.

The guys laughed at the other table, and then Mike pushed back his chair. He strolled over and slid into the seat next to Laura. "Hi, my name's Mike."

"I know. I'm Laura Newman." Laura's dark eyes never left his face. She was good at making a guy feel important.

"I know you, too," he said with a slow grin. "Who are your friends?"

"Suzanne and Amy," Laura told him. The two girls on the other side of the table waved.

Suzanne leaned close to Amy and whispered, "Do you think we should leave?"

Amy shrugged her shoulders. Laura didn't seem to mind the company, and Mike was so busy looking at Laura that it was hard to tell how he felt.

"I hear you like heavy metal." His full attention was on Laura, as though the other two girls had disappeared.

"Like it? I *love* it." No one could accuse Laura of being subtle.

"What about Cobra?"

Laura squeezed her eyes shut for just a second or two for effect. "They're my *favorite* next to Yellow Dog."

"Yellow Dog's hot," he agreed. "Were you at the concert Saturday?"

"Yeah. Third row."

He brushed his hand over his short hair. "I was fifteen rows back. Too bad I didn't see you there."

Laura gave him an impish smile. "That is too bad."

Mike blushed. Suzanne kicked Amy under the table and she knew what her friend was thinking. Mike Norton was getting ready to make a move. Amy had noticed long ago that spending time with Laura could actually be considered educational when it came to dealing with guys.

"I've got tickets for Cobra on Friday. Would you like to go with me?"

"That would be great!"

Amy shook her head. Laura had skipped school and waited three hours to get tickets for that concert. So far she hadn't been able to talk anyone into going with her. Now she would have to sell both of her tickets, but she hadn't hesitated for a moment over Mike's invitation.

Mike left after the two of them agreed on a time and Laura gave him her address. As soon as he was safely back at his own table, Amy noted, "I never knew you liked him."

"And you already had tickets for the concert," Suzanne added.

"Yeah. I have two tickets and I couldn't find a *close friend* to go with me. Now I can go with someone who really appreciates the music."

"What about your tickets?" Suzanne asked, worried.

Laura laughed. "Suzanne, you always get too involved in the technicalities. I'll sell them to a guy in my social studies class."

"The guy with the long hair and the bandanna who offered to buy one of your tickets and be your date?" Amy teased.

"I think he'll buy them." Laura obviously had no time for jokes. She had more serious business on her mind. "What should I wear?"

"Are you really worried about this date? I never heard you mention Mike before today," Amy said.

"Of course I'm worried. He's Scott Dunnel's friend," Laura explained as if Amy were an idiot. "I have to make the right impression."

"You're going to use him to meet Scott?" Suzanne sounded appalled.

Laura bristled. "I don't use people. I might meet Scott if I hang around with Mike. Or I might find out Mike is a great guy himself. After all, he likes Yellow Dog and Cobra."

"That would convince me," Amy joked.

"Funny, Tyler," Laura replied with a twinkle in her eyes. "We all know you would prefer someone with tickets to *Hello Dolly*."

Amy blushed. She was glad she always reacted that way when they teased her about being too conservative. They had no idea her face was turning red now because Laura had come so close to the truth. Amy knew what she wanted to be doing Friday night while her friend was getting her eardrums blown out by Cobra.

"I can get it!" Mrs. Tyler called when the doorbell rang at five-thirty.

Amy ran down the stairs from her bedroom and stumbled over her own feet at the bottom. Grabbing the railing, she was almost breathless. "That's okay, Mom. I think it's for me."

Her mother slid her glasses down her nose and peered over the top of them. "Expecting someone special?"

Amy wasn't quite ready to admit he was special. In fact, she was only ninety-nine percent sure she was going to accept the date with him. "Just the guy who's going to help me pass history this quarter," she quipped.

Her mother headed back into the kitchen where she was grading spelling tests at the table. Amy plunged her fingers into her hair to fluff up her hair as she walked to the door.

"Hi!" She had to smile when she saw Ben. He looked so cool in his leather bomber jacket.

"Good evening." He grinned and showed off the cute little space between his front teeth.

She took his jacket and hung it in the front closet. "Let's go in the living room. My mom is working in the kitchen."

He followed her into the room with the high-backed country plaid couch and love seat. "Sometimes my mom comes home and buries herself in fabric swatches. But how much work can a second-grade teacher bring home?"

"Only twenty-eight spelling tests." Amy rearranged the pillows on the love seat and sat at one end.

He sat at the other end and stretched out his legs. "She doesn't give them hard words, does she?"

"No, the hard part for her, though, is trying to read their printing." Amy laughed. Her mother loved her little pupils, but she always had funny stories to tell.

"I've had teachers say that's still a problem with my work except I've graduated from printing poorly to scribbling script even worse."

Amy liked sitting around talking with Ben,

but she reminded herself that he'd come for the six-hundred-page book she'd left on the end table. "Here's the book you wanted to use for our project."

He placed it on his lap and carefully opened to the table of contents. Then he flipped through a few pages. "This will be great. Have you decided who you want to be yet?"

"No, but I've read the pages on Bull Run in our class book." It was important to Amy that Ben understand she was willing to do as much as she could for their project, even if her best wasn't anywhere close to what he was planning to do.

"Do you want to be the winning or losing general?" he asked.

"I thought it might come down to who could do the better southern accent. After all, Beauregard was born in New Orleans," Amy said.

"You're the actress," Ben said. "Let's hear your best accent."

"Is this an audition?" Amy clasped her hands together and pretended to be very nervous.

"You could call it that," he said, going along with the joke.

Amy dropped her voice half an octave. "Well, then, General McDowell. I just think y'all should know my boys are gonna whup yours."

Ben raised his hands in surrender. "The part is yours!"

"You're not going to even give it a try?" Amy's mother asked from the archway that separated the small entry area from the living room.

"You sound like a teacher, Mrs. Tyler," he teased.

"How did you . . .?" She looked past Ben to Amy. "What else has my daughter told you about me?"

Ben slid the heavy book off his lap and jumped to his feet. "Only good things," he assured her. Offering his right hand, he politely said, "I'm Ben Richardson. Amy and I are doing a history project together."

"The Civil War," Mrs. Tyler said.

Amy smiled. Her mother was always friendly, but Amy had never had a boy in the house who fit in so easily.

Her mother shook her head and used her best schoolteacher's voice to say, "Are you sure you don't want to try for the Beauregard role?"

Amy wished he would try. She thought he was just being nice. Ben Richardson seemed like the kind of guy who would be good at everything.

He shook his head. "I want to be a reporter or newscaster, not an actor. I don't do impressions."

Amy's mother shook her head. "It looks like this guy has his heart set on being McDowell."

"A good man," Amy's father boomed, coming through the kitchen with his briefcase still in hand. It looked like he had just come home from the bank. He looked at Ben. "Are you Amy's friend who's going to borrow the history book?"

"Yes, sir." Ben extended his hand again, and Amy's mother said, "This is Ben Richardson."

Her father and Ben shook hands while Amy hung over the back of the love seat to watch the scene. Parents didn't seem to bother Ben in the least. Laura always had problems getting boys to meet her family.

"So you like history?" her father asked Ben.

"I'm most interested in the present . . . politics and stuff. But I think history could be a hobby someday."

"When you're out of school?" Amy's dad suggested. When Ben nodded, he added, "That's what happened to me. I liked history classes but they weren't very practical for a business major. I skipped the classes in college, but I read a lot now."

"It's probably better that way," Ben said. "You don't have to worry about grades."

Her father laughed, and Amy wished she could talk Mr. Wilson into letting her take history as a hobby. It might not be so bad if she didn't have to worry about her grade all the time.

Amy's mother took her father by the hand and tugged him toward the kitchen. "I have to tell you what happened to me today."

"Sometimes my dad gets pretty friendly, but my mom keeps him in line," Amy told Ben as he walked back to her.

Returning to his end of the love seat, Ben said, "I think they're both very nice."

Amy smiled. She liked them, too. "But my dad would have talked history with you for the next five hours. Once he gets started, it's impossible to stop him."

"Then I'm glad your mom took him into the kitchen." He rested his hands on top of the book he was borrowing. "I want to start reading this tonight. I'll get it back to you by the end of the week so you can read the parts you need over the weekend."

"Thanks." Amy felt guilty that he was doing so much work. "I could go to the library tomorrow and look up my man in the encyclopedia."

"That will give you some good background information," he said with approval.

"Should I check out your guy, too?" she offered. Ben smiled, and Amy felt good about contributing to their project.

"I'd appreciate it." He checked his watch. "I've got to be home in twenty minutes for dinner, and we haven't talked about Friday yet."

Amy bit her lip. A single brain cell somewhere in the back of her head still worried about Laura, but Amy knew her friend had new plans that didn't include Ben.

Ben leaned to one side and dug something out of his back pocket. "This isn't a bribe, but I have something for you."

Amy took the folded sheet of paper from him and opened it. She read the scribbled name twice before she covered her gaping mouth with her free hand. It couldn't be!

"Elle Rico was really nice when I picked her up yesterday," Ben explained. "I figured it wouldn't hurt to ask her for an autograph."

"I don't believe this," Amy said softly. "Thank you."

"You're welcome." He stared at the book sitting between them.

Amy realized he was embarrassed. He'd been so comfortable with her parents that she hadn't thought anything would bother him. "What time do you want to pick me up Friday night?" she said.

Chapter Five

Ben was in such a good mood when he came to pick up Amy on Friday night that she knew she'd made the right decision about going out with him.

"Have a good time tonight," her mother said as the pair started out the door.

"Ben, we want her home by midnight," Mr. Tyler told him in his fatherly voice.

Ben promised to bring Amy home before her chariot turned back into a pumpkin, and the Tylers laughed. As soon as they got outside, he whispered to Amy, "Have a good time but be home in five hours. It's a tough assignment, but I think we can do it."

At first she'd thought he was complaining about her curfew. When he turned it into a joke, she punched him in the arm with her mittened fist.

He grabbed nis arm as though he were seriously wounded. "General Beauregard, please! Save the battle for a week from Wednesday."

"Don't remind me," she groaned.

"I thought you liked our project," he said, holding the car door open while she slid into her seat.

As soon as he climbed behind the wheel, she tried to explain her feelings. "I think our project is the most interesting in the whole class. I'm just worried I won't be ready in time. I've never been very good in history. There's so much I need to find out."

"You'll do it," he said with confidence. "Why don't you put in a tape?"

Amy pulled off her mittens and looked through his cassette box. She grinned over at him. "You just want to show off the sound system you put in by yourself."

"Can I help it?" He shrugged. "It's the first time I ever did anything electrical. A friend helped me, but it's pretty exciting to do something like that and have it work."

"I'd be excited about it, too." Amy could understand his pride. "About the most mechanical thing I can do is put batteries in my radio."

"I have to learn to do these things if I want to keep this car in shape," he said. "Body shops are so expensive."

"Why don't you just get a newer car?" Amy wondered aloud. If his father were an important person at U.S. Electronics, they should have plenty of money.

"I don't want to have anything I can't pay for myself." Oncoming traffic threw some light into the car, and Amy saw the stubborn set of his jaw. "I want to be my own person."

"You sound serious." Personally, if her dad wanted to give her a car, or even approve a loan for her at the bank, Amy would be happy to accept the help.

"I have an older brother," he said suddenly. "They gave him a sports car when he graduated from high school. They're paying for him to go to Harvard. And he doesn't appreciate any of it. My parents don't say much about it, but I can tell it hurts them. I'm not going to do the same thing."

"Wow." Amy wasn't sure what else to say. His reasons were honorable, but she wondered if he weren't cheating himself.

He shrugged. "Where's that tape?" he asked. Amy realized he wanted to change the subject, so she grabbed the first one she found in the box and popped it into the player. Instead of music, though, Ben's voice came out of the speakers.

"What are citizens to do when their police can't protect them? Another shooting victim in Madison Park. What do we need vigilantes—"

Ben reached over and pushed the eject button. "We don't want to listen to that."

"What was it?" She grabbed the cassette from the player and tried to read the label. When they passed under a streetlight, she saw a date handwritten on the white tag. "Is this a class assignment or something?"

Ben concentrated on his driving, staring at the car in front of them. "You know I want to be a reporter or something . . ."

"Yeah." Maybe he'd made the tape for someone at the TV station.

"Well, I like to make tapes as if I'm reporting on real events. It's like practice." Ben shook his head. "It sounds stupid, right?'

"Not at all," she said firmly. Laura had made it sound bad when she described him as ambitious, but Amy admired his direction. "People who want to be musicians practice. Guys who want to play college or professional football play on the high school team. It's . . . good training."

He peered at her. "Are you kidding?"

Amy found another tape and made sure it was a musical one. "I'm not joking, Ben. I think it's great that you know what you want to do."

They got to the Playhouse just before the houselights dimmed. After Ben had helped Amy slip out of her coat, he rested his arm on the back of her seat. At first all she could think about was how close his arm was to her back and how well they got along. But when the pit orchestra began the overture, Amy was lost in the music. By the time the curtain went up, she leaned back in her seat and it didn't bother her at all when her hair brushed against Ben's arm. It felt right.

Amy felt a chill down her back when Nurse Nellie met Emile de Becque, and he sang "Some Enchanted Evening." When all the clapping died down, Ben leaned close to her.

"Remind you of the way we met?" he whispered.

Amy was glad for the darkness. It hid the blush that she felt creeping up her cheeks. There *had* been some kind of magic on that double date. Amy wondered if she should have realized back then that she wasn't the only one who had known it was special. If she had known Ben felt the same way she'd felt, what would she have told Laura?

Sometime after intermission, Ben's hand ap-

peared on the armrest between them. Casually
Amy set her hand next to his and waited for
something to happen. Moments later, he took
her small hand and cradled it in his. His hand
was warm but rough. She wondered if he'd gotten calluses from working on the car or doing
physical work at the television studio. She liked
the idea that he was his own person. Most of
the rich guys she'd met at Madison High lived
off their parents' money without giving it a second thought.

When Nellie the nurse turned her back on
Emile because she didn't understand his world,
Amy carefully slipped her hand away. She needed
it to wipe away the tears that were pooling in
her eyes. The way Nellie and Emile's relationship had begun so magically made their problems seem too sad.

Nellie realized what she could be losing when
Emile volunteered for a dangerous spy mission.
He rushed into her welcoming arms, and then
the play was over. Ben was quick to reach for
Amy's coat and help her into it. He waited until
they were outside, away from the crowd and in
the brisk night air, before he asked, "Do you
miss it?"

"Miss what?"

"Acting. I saw you getting misty when the

leading lady got the bouquet of roses." His arm went around her shoulder again. "Are you sorry it can't be you?"

She laughed happily. "I was just thinking how she must feel at the end of such a successful show. I wasn't jealous or wishing it was me."

"You're really not a frustrated actress?" He tipped his head as if trying to read her mind.

"No. I only tried out for the play last year because it sounded like fun. I like being involved in things."

"You like people," he added.

She gazed into his eyes, hoping to tell if he were guessing or if he honestly knew her that well already. The steady warmth in his amber eyes told her he knew a lot about her.

"Would you like to get a dessert at Confectionnaire?" he asked when they both were in the car.

"My parents have been there. My mom says the food is so wonderful it's decadent."

"Then let's do it! It's just a few blocks from here," he said quickly. He backed out of the parking spot and drove the short distance to the expensive French restaurant.

Amy's breath caught when they stepped inside. While Ben spoke to the maître d', she checked out the surroundings. It was absolutely beautiful. Delicate chandeliers hung in the center of the main dining room, throwing soft light on the pastel printed walls. As they walked to their table, she noticed the other diners were mostly adults in evening clothes. There was no chance anyone from the high school was going to see her with Ben and tell Laura. Maybe one of her friends' parents might be there, but they wouldn't be looking for her.

She hated to even think about Laura; the night was too special for her to worry about Laura popping up from a table and asking how Amy and Ben happened to be out together. Besides, Laura was on her own date. Amy opened a menu and sucked in her breath when she saw the prices.

"I know it's an expensive place," Ben said. "That's why I'm not buying you dinner."

"Sure I can get the Fudge Spécialité?" she teased. "I mean, I've got a few dollars if that would help."

"Wouldn't you be surprised if I borrowed it from you?" he countered.

"Honestly, Ben," she said seriously, "I like the way you handle being rich."

He looked up in surprise. "Most of the girls I dated back in Chicago thought I was silly. There was a rumor that they had a contest to see which girl could get me to spend the most money on her."

"That's terrible!" Amy thought they must have been awfully shallow girls not to see that he had made a decision to be independent and was trying to live up to it.

"Maybe you're just special," he said softly, just loud enough for Amy to hear him.

Ben walked her to her door ten minutes before midnight. He slid his hand from around her shoulders to the back of her neck. "Did I tell you how pretty you looked tonight?"

Amy swallowed hard and tried to tease him. "I think you forgot to mention that."

"I had a really good time tonight," Ben told her. "I hope you enjoyed yourself."

"I did," she whispered as he leaned closer toward her.

"I'm glad," he said as he closed the distance between them.

His mouth pressed against Amy's lips gently, and she felt her knees start to melt. But the kiss was over too quickly. She blinked, wondering if she'd done something wrong. "Is everything . . . okay?" she asked, barely finding her voice.

He gave her one of his lopsided grins and

tapped her nose with his index finger. "Everything seems perfect to me."

"Mom, do you have to go to class today?" Amy asked her mother the next morning.

Her mom stopped at the back door and adjusted her purse strap on her shoulder. "Is something wrong?"

Amy sighed. "I just wanted to talk."

"Could it wait?" her mother asked thoughtfully.

Amy loved it when her mom tried hard to be an ideal mother. Right now she was probably wondering whether or not her daughter would have permanent emotional scars if she went to her class. Amy didn't want her to worry. "It can be saved until you get home."

"Are you sure?" her mother persisted. Amy nodded, and her mother turned the door handle. "We'll talk later, but today the professor's supposed to give us a major assignment for this quarter, and I know I'll have questions."

Amy went back to bed, shaking her head. Why did her mother keep going to school when she didn't have to? She said it was important for her to keep up to date on new theories, but Amy thought her mother just liked being a student. Maybe she could talk her mom into going to Madison High for her someday when there was a test she wanted to avoid.

She was disappointed her mother had left. She was ready to burst from wanting to tell someone about her date. When she had first met Ben, and even when he had asked her out, she'd had no idea how much there was to learn about him, or how much she would like him once she got to know him better.

To be honest, she wasn't 'in the market' for a boyfriend. Like Suzanne, she dated quite often. Both of them had better luck with the guys they found on their own, as opposed to the dates Laura arranged for them, but things never worked out long-term for Amy. Sure, there had been a few guys who wanted to keep seeing her, but they had been so boring. And the couple of guys she wouldn't have minded sticking around with longer had developed other interests.

Suddenly it seemed like she'd found someone who felt the same way she did, and enjoyed the same things. She hadn't realized that until Ben made the comment about their 'magical" meeting during the song "One Enchanted Evening." Everything had changed somehow after he admitted how much he'd liked her since their first meeting. Laura often talked about magic, but Amy had never felt it until she met Ben.

Laura. This was the kind of thing best friends were made for . . . sharing wonderful news about dates. But Amy's palms got all sweaty when she thought about breaking the news to Laura. She wished with all her heart she'd told Laura everything from the beginning. Maybe Laura would have been disappointed, or even a little upset, but she wouldn't have held a grudge when she found out Ben was Amy's Mr. Right. Laura didn't even like him!

She decided to tell Laura the whole story. As soon as she found the nerve.

The phone next to her bed rang, and Amy had the hopeful thought it might be Ben. She tried her best to sound sexy. "He-llo?"

"Did I wake you up?" Laura asked with more energy than any human being should have on a Saturday morning after a late date.

"No. I was just lying around." Amy told herself this was her chance. She had to tell Laura about her evening.

"Good. I've got to tell you about last night. It is just too *fabulous* to be true," Laura chattered on.

"Why don't you come over?" Amy preferred to share her own news in person.

"Because I don't want to get out of bed. I'm

afraid if I get up and get dressed, last night might all turn out to be a dream."

"Was Cobra that good? Did you get invited backstage?"

"Better than that," Laura gushed. Amy couldn't imagine anything better than that from her friend's point of view until Laura explained, "Mike invited me to Scott Dunnel's party next weekend!"

Amy grinned at her words. The only thing that could top this on Laura's list of high school ambitions would be a date with Scott himself. An invitation to one of his parties was truly the kind of thing that Laura dreamed about. "Tell me all about it," Amy encouraged her friend, thinking how this was easing her worries about Ben.

Laura spent five minutes describing Mike's great car, fifteen minutes on the concert, and then it took a full half hour for her to repeat Mike's invitation word for word with every detail about his clothes and hair included. By the time she finished, Amy was exhausted.

Amy knew this wasn't the right time to tell Laura about Ben. She told herself she wasn't chickening out; there were plenty of reasons to keep the news to herself. Laura was so happy right now that she didn't want to ruin her best friend's high. Besides, it would be all wrong to do it on the phone. She had to see Laura to tell how her friend was taking the news. The expression on Laura's face would help Amy know how to handle the situation. Without that guide, she could really make a mess of her confession.

There would be a better time.

Chapter Six

On Tuesday afternoon, Amy was trying to remember whether or not she had any math homework when someone grabbed her shoulder from behind. She spun around quickly and accidently elbowed Ben in the stomach.

"Ben! I'm so sorry."

"Great to see you, too," he groaned.

Amy would have laughed at her clumsy mistake if Laura hadn't had the habit of always meeting her at her locker after school. While Ben clutched his abdomen, she looked past him for a sign of her friend.

"I think it would help if you had a drink of water," she advised, slamming her locker shut and hustling him around the corner to an out-of-sight water fountain.

71

He took a few sips and then collapsed against the cool wall. "Are you always this nice to guys that take you out?" he inquired, rubbing his stomach gently.

"Did I really hurt you?" With Laura out of her mind, she realized how uncomfortable he looked. His shoulders were sagging inside his open bomber jacket and his face was a little pale.

He grinned. "Just knocked the wind out of me, but I'm a tough guy."

"Sure. Do you have your car with you?" she inquired.

"Yeah." He rattled his keys in his pocket.

"Will you let me walk you to your car so I'll know you didn't faint in the parking lot?"

"I'd feel even better if you'd go to the Tiger's Den with me. I could use a Coke about now."

Amy reluctantly shook her head. The Tiger's Den would be a definite mistake. Even if Laura and Suzanne weren't there today, someone would tell them they had seen Amy with Ben Richardson. Besides, she had to be somewhere else in fifteen minutes.

"Oh. Why not?"

"On Tuesday afternoons I'm a volunteer at the Golden Oaks nursing home." She stuffed her hands in her jeans pockets and studied her running shoes. Boys didn't like to hear about the time she spent with old people.

"What do you do there?"

"Help out a little," she hedged, knowing he was just being polite.

"I told you more than that about my job at WMXX," he told her, sounding a little hurt.

"Well . . . I read magazine articles to a couple of blind women, and sometimes I help them write letters to their grandchildren."

Ben studied her face like someone who hadn't seen her before. "I could tell you were a nice person, but—"

"This is enough to gag you." She'd heard that quite often.

"I don't mean that at all," he said quickly and reached for her hand. "A lot of people talk about helping and caring for other people, but not that many people really do anything about it. I think you're great."

Amy flushed. Except for her parents and other relatives their age, no one had ever thought it was a good way for her to spend some of her free time.

"Could I get a rain check on the Coke?" he asked, lightening the mood.

"Sure." *Just as soon as I straighten things out with Laura,* Amy thought.

"I've got to get to work, too, if we're not going to the Tiger's Den," he told her. "They're trading offices at the station, and I have to be around to help move furniture. It could be a late night. But if I get off early enough, would you like to meet me at the basketball game tonight?"

She had no choice but to lie. She and Laura and Suzanne always went to the games together. She felt a deep pang of diappointment as she made her excuses. "You see, I have a lot of homework tonight, and . . ."

"You don't have many books," he said obser-vantly.

She looked at the single math book in her hand. "I forgot them in all the excitement."

"Let's go back to your locker and get what you need," he said.

Amy wasn't worried about him walking her back to her locker now. Laura never stuck around school this long unless she was dating a guy who played some sport. The only other book she really needed was her English assignment, *The Scarlet Letter,* but she grabbed three others to support her heavy homework claim.

Once she was bundled up and ready to leave, Amy glanced at her watch. "Oh, no! I'm going to be late."

"How do you get to Golden Oaks?"

"It's just five blocks from here. I walk."

"I could drive you. It's on my way to the studio," he assured her.

"If it's really not out of your way, I'd appreciate it." They didn't have many volunteers at the home, and she hated to miss a session or even be late.

He zipped his jacket and put an arm around her shoulder, resting it on top of her overstuffed backpack. In the car, Ben put his favorite Yellow Dog tape into the cassette player and told Amy to listen for the bass guitar, but the first song had barely started by the time they reached the nursing home.

"How will you get home?" he worried as she climbed out of the car. "It gets dark so early."

She leaned on the door and smiled at him. "My dad picks me up on his way home from work. Are you sure you're feeling well enough to go to work?" she asked, concerned about him in return.

He patted his stomach without flinching. "Good as new. No one will ever know I was attacked by Amy Tyler."

She held one mittened hand up to her lips. "Shh . . . They think I'm a nice kid around here."

"I think they're right."

"Amy! Why are you acting so nervous?" Laura queried as the girls settled into the bleachers in the Madison High gym later that night.

Amy craned her neck one last time before she sat down. If Ben were somewhere in the gym, she wanted to know exactly where he was; that way she'd know how much time she would have to escape or blurt out the story to Laura before he reached their spot six rows from the top.

"I think she's had a caffeine overload," Suzanne said.

"At that boring nursing home?" Laura asked. "They probably gave her warm milk."

"Give her a break," Suzanne scolded, trying to keep the peace as usual.

Amy couldn't risk the disaster of Ben sneaking up on her. She had to tell Laura and Suzanne how she and Ben had started seeing each other. She opened her mouth, but it was too dry for her to speak.

Laura raised a few inches off her seat to wave at someone halfway down the bleachers. Amy and Suzanne stretched to see who was so interesting. They should have known: Mike Norton . . . and Scott Dunnel.

"Isn't he cute?"

"Mike or Scott?" Suzanne asked.

"I think they're both pretty great," Laura said. Suzanne glanced at Amy and rolled her eyes.

Laura smoothed her short hair behind her ears, primping in case the guys should turn around to look at her again. "What should I wear to the party Friday night?"

"I'm lucky if I live until Friday," Suzanne moaned. "Since I failed today's English assignment, my mother will kill me."

Suzanne's mother was in public relations, and she thought everyone in the Hanes family should have a talent with words. Suzanne did not have that gift, but her mother refused to admit it.

"What happened in English?" Amy asked, putting her own concerns aside for a few moments.

"You didn't hear? I told everyone at the Tiger's Den." Suzanne took a deep breath before launching into her story. "Ms. Kopelski gave us a situation and told us to write about it . . . for the whole hour."

"Isn't that better than listening to her read aloud?" Usually Suzanne told them how half the class fell asleep while Ms. Kopelski bored them to death reading old classics in her dry, toneless voice.

"But you don't know the idea she gave us," Suzanne said insistently, truly worried about her grade and her mother. "She said to imagine that a friend of mine suddenly had all kinds of clothes or other things that she or he couldn't afford. We had to say how they got it, or how we would deal with it, or whatever else struck us as appropriate."

"What did you do?" Amy was curious, but Laura must have heard the whole story that afternoon. She was deaf to Suzanne's dilemma while she waved and grinned at the guys.

"How was I supposed to know what to do? I couldn't imagine either you or Laura with a stash in your bedroom."

"Well—"

"About Friday night," Laura interrupted. "Should I wear that pink sweater I bought on sale last week?"

"What would you wear with it?" Suzanne asked.

"Probably my little black miniskirt."

Suzanne nodded enthusiastically and then turned to Amy. "I mean, was I supposed to think my friend had shoplifted all those things?"

"Is that what you wrote?"

"No, I thought the friend could have inherited a stack of money and spent it all on herself."

"That would work," Amy said, glancing around the gym once again.

"But that would mean someone had to die,"

Suzanne protested. "If someone died and left you money, would you spend it all on yourself and all at once?"

They rose for the "Star-Spangled Banner," and all conversations were on hold until the tip-off. When the Madison Bulldogs got the ball, everyone waited for them to make the first score. With all eyes on the court, Amy clenched her fists and vowed to tell her story before Ben appeared on the scene.

As the ball cleared the hoop, Suzanne finished her story. "I couldn't kill off any of my friend's relatives, so I said the girl's parents were divorcing and the father had given her all the things, trying to buy her loyalty."

"That's good. You know I'm working on an interesting project in my history class—"

"You think the divorce thing was good? I can see Ms. Kopelski wanting to have a little talk about my family. I just hope she doesn't call my mother and ask if she's getting a divorce!" Suzanne twisted a strand of her long hair in distress.

"Have you heard about my history project?" Amy tried again.

"You hate history," Laura said emphatically.

"I used to, but we're doing this thing where

79

I'm going to be General Beauregard talking about how I won the Battle of Bull Run—"

"Are you sure the pink sweater will be okay?" When Amy made a face, Laura apologized. "I want to hear all about the war—after I settle this clothes thing. I was thinking I should buy something new."

Suzanne and Laura discussed what outfit would make the best impression. Then they talked about which stores had the best prices. Amy was wringing her hands by the time the other girls decided to go shopping after school the next day.

"Are you coming with us?"

"What time tomorrow?" Amy kicked Laura to remind her they were getting together to finish the plans for Suzanne's surprise party.

"That's right. I've got an appointment in the afternoon," Laura said, recovering very well. "Let's shop after dinner."

"Count me out." Amy was disappointed, but she knew she had too much work to do tomorrow. "I've got an English test on Friday. And I've only read half the book so far."

Laura had another concern. "How can I get Mike into the house to meet my parents Friday night?"

"He didn't meet them last time?" Suzanne asked.

"No, and my dad's pretty hot about it. He likes to meet my dates."

"My parents sure liked—" Amy blushed at her blunder and concentrated fiercely on the court below.

"I'm afraid they won't let me see him again if I don't drag him into the house!"

Amy tried to bring Ben into the conversation two more times before the group fought their way to the concession stand in the lunchroom at halftime. It was impossible to have a serious conversation in the crowd, but Amy finally felt safe. There was no way Ben or anyone else would be able to find her in that mess.

"Look who's here," some guy near them called.

Laura flashed her brightest smile. "Hi, Mike. Hi, *Scott*."

"Why do you sit so far up?" Mike asked.

"It's a better view," she told him, instead of saying that the seats had been the best the three of them could get their freshman year. They had sort of adopted that row.

"Would you like to sit with us?"

Amy saw Laura's eyes glaze for half a second. Sitting in Scott Dunnel's group at a basketball game was probably enough to make Laura faint. Amy was ready to catch her friend if she swooned.

"Is there room for me?" Laura asked sweetly.

"We'll make room," Mike announced.

Laura looked at her friends, her dark eyes pleading for their understanding. "You guys don't mind, do you?"

Amy didn't have the heart to remind her that they always sat together, and Suzanne must have felt the same way. She just said, "Have fun."

In the second half, their special spot felt a little empty without Laura. "I hope she's having a good time," Amy said, glancing down at the popular crowd.

"Are you kidding? She probably thinks she's died and gone to heaven," Suzanne joked. More seriously, she added, "I don't know why we put up with her."

"Sure you do, we're friends." It was so simple in Amy's mind. "She stuck with me in eighth grade when I decided to be a scientist. She didn't even laugh when I turned my shoes green when I spilled that chemical on them during an experiment. She still liked you when you threatened to never talk to us again if you made the cheerleading squad. It's our turn to be there for her."

"But she's been boy-crazed a lot longer than you were a chemist. And I never made the cheerleading squad," Suzanne pointed out.

"But she's still the same person underneath. She still cares about us," Amy insisted. At least she hoped that was true.

Amy grew silent as she realized that if she didn't tell Laura about Ben soon, it might be too late. Laura might find Amy and Ben together the next time Ben came to her locker. Even if she didn't find out by herself, Laura might ask why Amy had waited so long to mention she'd been seeing Ben since two days after the Yellow Dog concert.

On the other hand, Laura might just laugh at the whole thing. Amy had seen her do it before. After all, she did have an intense crush on someone else, so why should she care? It was possible that Amy was worrying over nothing. She crossed her fingers, hoping she was right.

Chapter Seven

"That's what I'll do!" Amy said under her breath.

"Tyler!" her teammates screamed.

She looked up just in time to see the volleyball flying toward her face. Instinctively her hands popped up, and she hit the ball with her palms. The girl in front of her helped it over the net.

"Where's your head?" the girl next to her asked.

Solving my biggest problem, she answered to herself. Amy wasn't going to have to throw herself on Laura's mercy and admit she had been seeing Ben. Not if her new plan worked.

All she had to do was wait for Ben to ask her out again. Then she would phone Laura and pretend this was the first time Ben had called her since the concert. She'd had plenty of time to cool down since the Yellow Dog concert, and now she was dating Mike . . . and hanging around with Scott Dunnel's crowd. She wouldn't have any reason to be upset about Ben. In fact, Laura would probably offer her some advice on how to handle her *first* date with Ben Richardson.

Amy could see only one potential problem. Ben had to ask her out again for the plan to work. On the other hand, if Ben never asked her out again, she'd be upset about a lot more than Laura.

"Amy!" the other girls yelled.

She blinked. "What?"

"It's your serve."

Amy took her place at the line and launched the ball over the net. Her head was so full of her plan that she couldn't concentrate on the game. She knew she had to be careful about what she said to Laura between now and whenever Ben asked for another date. Her wonderful solution would be ruined if she let anything about the history study sessions or the play slip during a conversation.

"Can't you bring something besides your Yellow Dog and Cobra tapes?" Amy asked Laura later that afternoon.

"I don't have any Barry Manilow," Laura teased, lounging comfortably on the couch in the Tyler living room. "Besides, we have to listen to the radio part of the time. The KWAK disc jockey promised to mention Suzanne's birthday just before midnight."

"Okay." Amy checked off the KWAK job on the list of things they had to do before they were ready for the party.

"Aren't you impressed?" Laura inquired, her lower lip pushing out into a pout.

"Sure it's great." Amy said automatically, slightly annoyed. She wanted to get through the things on her list and send Laura home. She knew the longer they were alone together, the more chances she would have to say something wrong . . . something that would ruin her plan.

Amy tapped her pencil on the list of things to do. "What about the food?"

"You're getting the chips and dip," Laura said. "And I'm in charge of popcorn."

"We'll order pizza around midnight." Amy thought they were pretty well organized. Suzanne was usually in charge of things like this, but they could hardly have asked her to coordinate her own surprise birthday party.

"And I'll be over Saturday afternoon to help with the cake," Laura insisted.

"Okay." Amy checked her list and nodded. "Anything else we need to cover?"

"What's your hurry?"

The back door closed and Amy used it as an excuse not to answer Laura's question. "Mom? Is that you?"

Her mother came into the living room. "Hi, sweetheart. Hi, Laura. Are you girls working on the big party?"

"We're trying to," Laura said with frustration in her voice.

"Is there a problem? Can I help?" Amy's mother offered.

"Everything's going just the way we planned," Amy insisted. "In fact, I think that's it," she said with finality.

Laura stood up and reached for her jacket. "I guess we're done. But I don't know why we had to rush through it."

"Homework," Amy said simply. "I'm drowning. I've got a test Friday on *The Scarlet Letter*—which I haven't finished yet. And I've got to work on my history project . . ."

"Is Be—"

"Not to mention my math assignment," Amy said quickly, cutting off her mother's question.

Laura slipped into her jacket. "Suzanne and I'll be thinking about you while we're shopping tonight for my outfit for Friday."

"I hope you find something perfect." Amy felt a little guilty about chasing her best friend out of the house, but she was scared to death her mother might say something about Ben.

When the back door closed behind Laura, Mrs. Tyler went upstairs to change into something more comfortable than her teaching clothes. Amy flipped on the television and curled up on the love seat to watch an afternoon talk show.

"I thought you had tons of homework," her mother said when she came through the living room on her way to the kitchen.

"I'll get to it."

"You're not really drowning, are you?" her mother asked.

"Not exactly," Amy admitted.

"Is there something going on between you and Laura?"

"I'm handling it." Amy wanted to feel like she was in charge.

"That's good. But could I help?" her mother

asked. "You and Laura have been close friends for so long that I'd hate to see you having problems."

"It's about a guy," Amy admitted, turning off the television.

"I should have known. Nothing causes more problems for friends than men," her mother said with a laugh. She walked toward the kitchen. "Have a snack with me, and we'll talk."

Mrs. Tyler dished up applesauce for both of them. "What's the deal? Do you have a crush on one of Laura's guys? Or did some guy she likes have the nerve to be interested in you?"

"It's Ben."

Her mother dropped her spoon. "Ben Richardson? He seems so nice. How can he be a problem?"

"Ben's wonderful," Amy said, jumping to his defense.

"Does Laura think he's wonderful, too?" her mother asked, trying to figure out what was happening between the two girls.

Amy shook her head. "Laura doesn't like him."

"Ahh . . ." Her mother nodded as if the whole thing were suddenly clear to her. "You like Ben, but your friends don't approve."

"No," Amy sighed deeply. "They don't even know about him."

Mrs. Tyler squinted across the table at Amy. "I'm confused. Please start at the beginning."

"It started with the Yellow Dog concert." Amy felt strange, finally talking about Ben and Laura.

"The blind date?" When Amy nodded, her mother added, "I didn't think Ben was your date."

"He wasn't. He was Laura's date."

"Ooh . . ."

"Don't say that," Amy said firmly. "I didn't steal him from Laura, if that's what you're thinking. He was just very nice to me at the concert."

Mrs. Tyler rinsed her applesauce bowl and took some chicken out of the refrigerator to start fixing dinner. "How did Laura feel about that?"

"She was really upset."

"I bet she was," her mother said with a laugh.

"It's not what you're thinking. She never liked Ben—she just wanted to see Yellow Dog—but it hurt her pride when he seemed to like me better than her."

Her mother chuckled as she held the chicken pieces under running water at the sink. "Considering how Laura feels about guys, I'd guess she was very angry."

"We talked about it and decided we didn't

really have a problem because I'd probably never see Ben again."

"But you did," her mother pointed out.

"I didn't plan it," Amy insisted. "He showed up in my history class the next Monday, and we decided to be partners for the Civil War project."

"Didn't you think that would bother Laura?"

"Who's side are you on?" Amy asked.

"Amy, I'm your mother. I am always on your side, but I'm trying to understand what has happened."

"I thought about Laura a little bit, but it didn't seem wrong to accept his help with history. You know what kind of grades I usually get in that class." It had seemed so simple back then.

"So you were just going to be partners on the project," her mother repeated.

"Right, just a school assignment. But then we started working together and I found out what a special person he is. Then he asked me out. What was I supposed to do? I *wanted* to go to the play with him."

"I think you should have accepted. But I also think you should have told Laura what was going on," her mother said bluntly.

"I tried to . . ."

Amy's mother looked over her shoulder and raised her eyebrows in a challenge.

"I really did," Amy protested. "Laura called me the next morning and I wanted to tell her about my date, but she was so full of news about her night that I didn't get a chance. Then I tried to tell her at the basketball game, but she was too interested in Mike."

"And those were your only two chances?" her mother asked in disbelief. "What about this afternoon, or any other afternoon for that matter?"

"Okay," Amy said in surrender. "I could have found a time to tell her, but I was afraid she'd get mad at me."

"So you kept putting it off."

"And the longer I waited, the more I had to tell her . . . and the more upset I thought she would be." Amy didn't like facing the truth. She could have told Laura if she had really wanted to; instead, she'd been looking for excuses.

"What are you going to do? Go over to her house right now and tell her, or wait even longer and make it even worse?"

"Neither."

"Neither?" Her mother wiped her hands and came back to the table. "Things are getting tense between you and Laura. You can't pretend the problem's going to go away if you ignore it."

Amy crossed her arms on the table. "I'm not ignoring it. I have a better idea."

"I can't wait to hear it."

"When Ben asks me out again, I'm going to tell Laura about it like it's our first date," Amy explained. "Since she's involved with a new guy now, I don't see why she should care."

Her mother sighed and shook her head sadly. "A lie? When has a lie ever been the best way to solve a problem?"

"It will be this time," Amy said, enthusiastically defending her plan. "Why should I hurt Laura by telling her about the past when it's not necessary?"

"I just don't know," her mother said softly. "Lies never seem to work. You get all tangled up in them and then they slap you in the face when you least expect it. All I can tell you, Amy, is that I wouldn't do it if I were you."

"But it *will* work." Amy was sure of it.

"Amy! Someone's here to see you!" Mrs. Tyler called up the stairs after dinner.

Amy left her copy of *The Scarlet Letter* facedown on her bed and galloped down the stairs. Laura was probably stopping by after her shopping trip to show off the perfect outfit she'd found for Scott's party.

Amy reached the bottom of the stairs and froze. "Ben. I didn't know you were coming over tonight."

He grinned. "I was just in the neighborhood."

She didn't believe that for a minute. He lived miles away from her, and the television studio wasn't anywhere near her house. She wished he had called; she looked a mess. Her mascara was probably smudged under her eyes, and Amy knew the gravy spot from dinner was still on her sweater. She hadn't bothered to change before tackling her homework.

"Could we sit down?" he asked.

"Sure."

He sat right in the center of the love seat, so Amy had to either sit close to him or on another piece of furniture. She chose to squeeze between Ben and the arm of the love seat.

"How's your history research going?"

"Did you come over to check up on me?" she teased. "Don't worry. I've started to write my part for the presentation."

"Will you be ready by next Wednesday?"

"I will," she promised, curious about the real reason for his visit. He could have asked her these questions in class tomorrow.

"Are you going to be studying Friday night?" he asked.

"Not if I can help it," Amy said with a grin. She believed in taking some time off from schoolwork over the weekend.

"Good." He looked into her eyes. "Would you like to go to a party with me at Scott Dunnel's house?"

The blood pounded in her ears at his words. She couldn't face him. Concentrating on the plaid pattern on the arm of the love seat, Amy could only think that Laura would be at the party. Her friend was so excited about Scott's party that she didn't want to spoil it for her— and showing up at the party with Ben might completely ruin Laura's evening.

"Hey, I know it's pretty late notice," he said when she didn't give him an answer. "I thought I had to do something with my parents Friday night, but I got out of it."

Amy wanted so much to go with him. He had to think she was pretty special to ask her to be his date at Scott's party. But when she'd come up with the plan to tell Laura that her next date with Ben was her first date with him, she hadn't expected the date to be such a big event. This wouldn't be the right time.

"Is something going on that I should know

about?" Ben asked, looking confused and a little hurt.

Amy gulped, hoping with all her heart he didn't have ESP or any other powers that would let him read her mind.

"Wh—what do you mean?"

"You never just agree to do things." He rubbed his chin. "But you seem to like me. Ever since the play—"

"I didn't know what my parents might have planned for that night," she interrupted, surprised he was bringing up their first date.

"And then you wouldn't go to the Tiger's Den with me." He ticked off the second example on his fingers.

Amy thought he was being unfair. "I was supposed to be at the nursing home."

"Okay. What about the basketball game?" He touched his third finger as if the charges against her were adding up.

Amy's breath caught in her throat. Had he seen her there? "I thought you had to work."

"I did. I worked until ten o'clock last night." The fact didn't seem to make him any happier. "It doesn't change the strange feeling I have right now. I thought you wanted to hang around with me, but maybe I've made a mistake."

"No!" she said quickly. She had made some

mistakes, but Ben was right to think she wanted to be with him.

He laid a hand on her right shoulder. "Tell me the truth, Amy. Don't you want to be seen with me? Do I embarrass you? Or do you have another boyfriend?"

Amy stared at him, her eyes wide with fear. She didn't want to tell him about Laura, but if she didn't, he was going to walk out of her house and probably never come back.

Chapter Eight

"There's something I have to tell you," Amy said softly, deciding she would rather explain what was really going on than let Ben think she didn't like him.

Ben leaned back against the couch cushions, but the firm line of his jaw told Amy he wasn't relaxing. "I've got time."

"Laura is going to be at Scott's party . . . and she doesn't know I've been spending time with you." Amy sat tensely on the edge of the couch, waiting for Ben to react to her terrible confession. She couldn't bear to look him in the eye. She was sure he'd hate her now that he knew how badly she'd treated her best friend.

After an excruciating silence, Ben shifted on

the couch. "What are you talking about?" he asked, dismayed.

Amy was surprised that he sounded more concerned and confused than angry. Then she realized she hadn't really explained anything at all. She'd have to try again.

"I never meant to hide anything from Laura," Amy said. "But she was really upset about the Yellow Dog concert." She was rambling, but at least in the right direction.

"Why?" Each thing she said seemed to confuse Ben more.

"Because you paid more attention to me than to her, and she was supposed to be your date." Amy was beginning to feel exasperated with the whole situation. It was so embarrassing.

"But she didn't want to talk to me," he said, defending his actions. "She only went with me to get to the concert. Besides, I liked you better."

Amy smiled in spite of herself. "Thanks."

"So does Laura hate me? Or did she make you promise not to see me again?" he inquired.

"Well . . ." Amy paused a moment to mull things over. "Laura was really mad at me the morning after the concert. At first I didn't know why—then I realized the whole thing had really wounded her pride. She sort of did ask me not to go out with you because she was afraid peo-

ple would think you'd dumped *her* to see me."
Amy let out a long sigh and slumped back into
the couch.

"So did you agree to it . . . to not going out
with me?" Ben asked with intensity.

"I didn't know what to do," Amy said. "I honestly never expected to see you again, and I was
sure you'd never just *call* to ask me out. Of
course, that was before history class."

"And then I did ask you out," Ben offered.

"And I said yes." Amy smiled a little despite
her misery.

"But you didn't tell Laura," Ben finished.

"No." Amy was quiet a long time. Ben reached
over and squeezed her hand.

"I guess I didn't tell her before the date, because she'd tell me not to go," Amy admitted,
finally being honest with herself about her silence. "And afterward she was so excited about
Mike and Scott—two new guys she has crushes
on—that I didn't want to spoil her mood."

"Why don't you tell her tomorrow—or even
call her tonight—so we can go to the party Friday night?" Ben suggested as if it would be the
easiest thing in the world.

"Because I have another plan." He raised his
eyebrows just as her mother had done, and
Amy took a deep breath before explaining her

idea. "I could call Laura and tell her you invited me to the party, pretending it was the first time I've heard from you since the concert."

"You'd do that?" he asked in disbelief.

"If you'll help me. I mean, we'd have to be careful not to mention the play in front of her."

"Or the history project, or the ride to Golden Oaks, or the autograph I got for you. Are you willing to forget the time we've spent together already?" Ben seemed upset.

"I'm not asking you to forget it." She certainly wouldn't forget a second of the time they'd had together since they met at the concert. "I'm just asking you to help me."

"I can't do it," he said with finality.

"Why not? If you'd help me, we could go to the party."

"And turn our relationship into a lie," he concluded. "What we have . . . and what we could have . . . is too special to risk for a stupid game."

When Ben suggested they could have a future together, Amy got chills down her back, but she also sensed the tension and disappointment in his voice. Obviously he'd expected her to be above the sort of games Laura played all the time.

"I don't know how else to handle the situation," she whispered.

"It's simple," Ben said. "Talk to Laura. I don't see why she should care now. She already has another boyfriend, right?"

"But I can't," Amy said, honestly convinced it would be impossible. "Laura would have been mad enough if I'd told her at the beginning, but now she'll be even more upset because I've been keeping it from her." Amy felt so miserable that she wanted to cry. She wanted Ben to take her in his arms and tell her they'd just skip the party.

Instead he said, "Amy, I know this is tough on you, but the party means a lot to me. I'll finally get a chance to get to know some more people here. I'll be part of the crowd instead of an outsider."

Amy looked at Ben. Of course he was right. How stupid of her to have forgotten his position in all of this. She'd talk to Laura.

"If I tell her," Amy said with a grimace, "she might be so angry that I won't be able to go to the same party as her. If I don't tell her, I can't go because she'll make a scene when she sees us together . . . and I'll disappoint you."

"Let's just see how Laura takes the news," Ben said, smiling. He wrapped his arm around her and gave her a hug. "Now, what about our history project?"

Ben's hand made slow circles on Amy's back as they talked about the history assignment. Finally Amy relaxed and forgot about Laura. The project demanded her full attention. Forty-five minutes later, Amy reluctantly walked Ben to his car.

"I know you can do it," he whispered in her ear as he pulled her close.

"I hope you're right," she replied. Then they kissed good-night. As their lips parted, Amy realized Ben was definitely worth the terrible time she was going to have telling Laura about them.

"Have you told her yet?" Ben asked Amy after their history class the next day.

"No, we're meeting at the Tiger's Den after school."

He leaned against the lockers and tried to cheer her up. "If you like, I can stop by tonight to see how it went . . . and so we can make plans for the weekend."

Ben seemed so relaxed. Amy tried to calm down, but she was too nervous. She had to keep one toe tapping or else she thought she would explode. Leaning to one side, she saw Laura coming in her direction.

"Behind you," she whispered to Ben. "You have to get out of here."

"What?"

She didn't have time to explain why he should disappear into thin air.

"Amy!" Laura called. She was still behind Ben but getting closer by the second. "I had to find you to discuss a few last-minute things about Suzanne's—"

Amy's heart plunged to her knees, and Ben rolled his eyes toward the ceiling. They had been caught. Amy's worst nightmare was coming true.

"Ben Richardson!" Laura cried. She seemed almost pleased to see him at first. Then her face changed as she looked from Ben to Amy and back again.

"Laura, I—"

"Don't tell me it's nothing, Amy Tyler," she spat. "You should see your face. You wouldn't be blushing redder than an apple if nothing was going on!"

Laura spun around and pushed her way through the crowded hall, going against the traffic flow. Amy watched until her friend was out of sight.

Ben expelled a big puff of air and began to stroke the hair at her temple. "Are you going to be all right?"

"She'll probably be at the Tiger's Den after

school, telling Suzanne how awful I've been. I'll try to talk to her there," Amy said in a shaky voice.

"I'm sorry, Amy."

She tried to smile into his worried face, but she just couldn't do it. Voicing the hope in her heart, she said, "I'll be okay."

"Hey, if you don't think you can face the rest of the day, we can go somewhere and talk."

He couldn't possibly know how tempting the suggestion was to Amy. She wasn't sure how she was going to sit through three more classes, but she had to stay. "I'd love to get out of here, but I can't. We're reviewing for tomorrow's English test, and I need the review."

"Okay." He hugged her. "I'll be thinking about you."

Just as she expected, Laura and Suzanne were huddled together in a booth near the back of the Tiger's Den after school. Her knees were actually shaking as she approached them.

"Can I sit down?" she asked hesitantly.

Laura looked up with a glare that made Amy half wish she'd never heard of Ben Richardson. Her throat went dry and she couldn't ask again. Luckily Suzanne spoke for Laura.

"Sure. If you want to . . ."

Amy slid into the seat opposite the other two girls. She took her time slipping out of her jacket and nestling her purse and backpack into the corner. After taking a deep breath, she said, "Laura, I was going to tell you about it this afternoon. Maybe that sounds a little convenient, but it's true."

"And what were you going to tell me? Do you expect me to believe this afternoon was the first time he had seen you since the concert?" Without giving Amy a chance to answer either of the questions, she continued, "Because I know a few things about guys, and Ben looked very comfortable with you. Guys aren't that relaxed around girls unless they know them pretty well—"

"Or unless there's nothing going on between them and they're just talking." Suzanne offered.

Amy detected a hopeful tone in Suzanne's voice, and she knew her friend wanted her to say it had been the first time she had run into Ben since the concert. She hated to disillusion Suzanne almost as much as she dreaded telling the whole truth to Laura.

Amy bit her lip. "Laura's right. I have been seeing Ben."

"How long?" Laura nearly choked on the question.

"It's not like I planned it. He's in my history class." Amy didn't even try to make excuses. Laura was really angry, and somehow she got smarter when she was mad. At times like this, Laura could see through even the best lies.

"You mean you've seen him every day since the quarter started . . . and you never mentioned it?" Laura's mouth fell open as if the truth were even more unbelievable than she'd expected.

"Yes." Amy stared at the table. "I can't help who's in my class."

"Is that all you have to say?"

"What do you want from me, Laura?" Amy was frustrated. "I could tell you it started because I had to be his partner on the Civil War project. In case you're interested, I'm finally going to get a decent grade in history, for once. I could tell you I hadn't mentioned our date because you were so excited about your first date with Mike that there was no room in the conversation for *my* news—"

"Are you trying to make this my fault?" Laura protested before the full meaning of Amy's words hit her. "Your date? You've gone out with him?"

"Just once . . . so far." Amy wasn't quite sure why she added the *so far*, except that she didn't plan to stop seeing Ben just because the situation with Laura had blown up in her face.

Laura ran her fingers over her slicked-back hair and then clasped her hands on the table. "You've been lying about everything," she said in utter disbelief.

"I never lied," Amy said, getting technical. "Maybe I didn't mention a few things, but I kept trying to find a way to tell you about him."

Laura sputtered, and Suzanne took advantage of the opening in the conversation. "I don't want to be unfair, Amy, but it is a little hard to believe you have been trying to tell Laura. You must have had a hundred chances."

"I suppose," Amy admitted unwillingly. "But it got harder each day. At first I didn't mention he was in my history class because Laura was still so mad about him. Then he asked me out, and how was I supposed to explain *that,* since I hadn't told you guys Ben and I had been working on our project? Afterward, how was I going to tell you about my date when you didn't even know I'd had one?" Amy stopped. She had always thought a perfect time would come. Instead, each day she'd waited had guaranteed Laura would be angrier when she found out the truth.

"You're right about all that," Laura said cynically. "I would have been mad if you'd told me you were his history partner. But I might have understood that . . ."

"Are you saying that if I'd told you sooner, you wouldn't have minded when it turned into more than just history partners?" Amy thought it was really mean of Laura to hint this whole disaster could have been avoided that easily.

"Sure I would have minded. But it wouldn't have hurt me as much as all the lies."

"I never lied to you. I never told you I wasn't seeing him," Amy insisted.

Laura sighed, and the fire in her eyes faded into pain. "Whether or not you lied, I feel betrayed. I thought we were best friends. I don't understand how you could have done this to me."

Were best friends? The idea sent a shiver down Amy's back. After all they had been through, she couldn't believe Laura was going to say they couldn't be friends anymore.

"C'mon, Laura," Suzanne said, clearly as shaken as Amy. "We've stuck together through the rumors Molly McNeil spread about you last year, and my swelled head when I thought I was going to be a cheerleader. You can't let Ben break up this group. We've got history."

"But none of us has done anything this terrible to the others before. I'm not sure I can forget it," Laura said honestly.

"Be fair," Suzanne encouraged her. "It's not so terrible. You didn't even like Ben, and you've got a new boyfriend now anyway. Keeping quiet about Ben wasn't the smartest choice Amy could have made, but she didn't keep him a secret just to make you feel bad any more than she started seeing him because she wanted to hurt your feelings. It just happened."

For the first time since Laura had caught Ben with her in the hall, Amy felt the knot in her stomach loosen. Suzanne understood. She hadn't intended to hurt anyone, but everything had turned into a mess that she couldn't control. Under the table, Amy crossed her fingers that Laura was really listening to Suzanne.

"I guess you're right," Laura said after thinking it over. "Our friendship is too special to let a guy ruin it."

"Thanks." Amy sighed with relief, not quite able to believe Laura's mood change.

"Don't you feel the same?" Laura asked Amy. "Wouldn't you choose our friendship over Ben Richardson?"

"Excuse me?" Amy didn't understand what Laura was getting at. Her friendship with the

111

other girls had nothing to do with her relationship with Ben.

"If you had to choose between Ben and us, who would you pick?" There was a steely look in Laura's dark eyes.

"Are you saying I have to make a choice?"

"No," Suzanne said, giving Laura a stern look. "Amy can still see Ben."

"Not if she wants to still hang around with me," Laura said firmly, meeting Suzanne's frown with a stare of her own. "How can I forget what has happened if I see him every time I turn around?"

"You have to be kidding," Amy said breathlessly. Her brain was spinning. The idea of not staying with Ben long enough to see what might happen between them made her heart ache. But the thought of facing school, weekends, and every other part of her life without Laura and Suzanne was inconceivable. Maybe all this would blow over when Laura had a chance to calm down.

"This isn't a joke, and I'm not going to change my mind," Laura said as if she'd read Amy's thoughts. "It's Ben or me. Which is it going to be?"

There really wasn't any choice to be made. How could she give up a friendship that had been the most important thing in her life since middle school for a guy she had known only two weeks? But this was so unfair.

"Can I see Ben just one more time?" she asked softly. When Laura grumbled under her breath, Amy hurried on to explain. "I have to try to make him understand. I don't want to hurt him."

Amy knew that was one of the most ridiculous things she had ever said in her life. There was no way she could tell Ben she was giving him up for Laura without hurting him. And without hurting herself.

Chapter Nine

"You can't read much that way," Mr. Tyler said to Amy as he passed through the living room after dinner.

"What?" Amy looked up at him from her prone position on the couch.

"It's hard to read when the book is lying face-down over your stomach, isn't it? Or have they developed some new study techniques at your school?" he teased.

"I'm not in the mood for jokes," she told him quietly. "I have a test in English tomorrow, but I couldn't tell you what's happening in this book."

"You'll be all right," he said, giving her an awkward pat on the arm before he went upstairs.

She knew her mother had told him about the

Laura and Ben disaster. How was she supposed to study when Ben would be ringing that doorbell any minute and she would have to tell him she was trading him in for Laura? Frustrated, she threw *The Scarlet Letter* on the floor and flung her arms over her face. Lying around on the couch since dinner wasn't doing much for her mood, but she didn't want to deal with the thoughts racing around in her head.

The doorbell rang, and Amy's mom peeked around the corner. "Do you want me to answer the door?"

Slowly, Amy swung her feet off the couch. "No, I'll get it."

Her legs seemed to be made of lead as she walked across the room. She had no idea how she was going to tell Ben.

He studied her face when he came into the house. "You look like you had a rough day," he said tenderly before he leaned down and kissed her on the forehead.

His kindness made Amy feel like a snake. Ben had come over to offer her sympathy. He had no idea what she was going to tell him.

"Let's sit down and talk," he said, leading her into the living room. Ben noticed the book lying on the floor. "I see you couldn't study either."

"You mean you've been . . . distracted, too?"

Amy had a hard time imagining Ben sitting around his house like a zombie.

"Sure, I was worried about you." He sat on the couch and pulled her down beside him. "Tell me what happened. Did you talk to Laura?"

"Yeah. I talked to her," Amy muttered.

"It doesn't sound like things went too well."

He took her hand and squeezed it, telegraphing his feelings to Amy. Even without words, she knew he was telling her to cheer up because he was still her friend. His tenderness and caring was making her feel worse than ever.

"If you want to talk about it, I'm here to listen."

Each thing he said to make her feel better only sent Amy's spirits lower. When she finished telling him the things she had to say, he was going to wish he hadn't invited her to share the news about Laura.

"She was really mad," Amy began.

"I thought she would be, considering how she looked when she found us together after history," he said.

"She hadn't cooled down any by the time I found her and Suzanne at the Tiger's Den." At least Ben understood how deeply Laura had been hurt. "She said I had lied to her."

"Did you?"

117

"Not technically. I just didn't tell her about you, but from her point of view it felt the same as if I had lied." Thinking about it after the argument at the Tiger's Den, Amy had seen Laura's point. It really didn't matter whether or not she had lied to Laura; what counted was that her friend felt betrayed.

"Did you explain the situation to her? Did you tell her our dating hadn't been your idea?" he asked. "I mean, it's not like you chased me or something."

"I tried to explain everything." Amy sighed in defeat as she remembered offering her reasons. She still didn't believe she had done anything as bad as Laura made it sound, but that didn't matter now.

"Are you and Laura still friends?" he asked cautiously.

Amy bit her lip. She couldn't put off telling him any longer, but she didn't want to see the look on his face when she told him what she had agreed to do to keep the friendship together.

"What is it?" His voice and eyes reflected his concern. "Did she tell you to drop off the face of the earth?"

"Worse," Amy whispered. "She told me I couldn't see you anymore."

Ben squinted at her. "What do you mean? How can she stop us from being together?"

"If I don't stop seeing you, then she won't be my friend," Amy told him with no emotion in her voice. She felt as if someone else had spoken the words, as if someone else were watching Ben shake his head as he began to understand.

"She gave you an ultimatum?" He was stunned.

Amy nodded, unable to find her voice.

"Who did you . . ." He stopped and swallowed very hard. "What have you . . . decided?"

She could tell he hated asking the question. Ben knew her well enough to know how much she valued Laura's friendship.

"Laura and I go back to middle school," she told him, trying not to listen when he sucked in a deep breath. "I've only known you two weeks."

"So we're supposed to forget the good times we've had together and not think about what could have happened between us?" he asked angrily. "Who does she think she is, anyway?"

Amy rubbed her temples. It seemed as though all she had done that day was argue with people. Fighting with Laura had exhausted her. Just thinking about having to face Ben had drained her emotionally. She didn't have the energy left to debate him.

"I know this has been hard on you," he said

119

wihout the sympathy he'd had earlier. "But this is important to me. Are you willing to throw it all away?"

She looked him in the eye and the hardness in his gaze made her heart ache. "I don't want to do this, but I don't really have a choice."

He reached for her shoulders and held onto her tightly. "Look, I know you're not going to give up your best friend for me. But isn't there some way to talk Laura out of this?"

Amy shook her head miserably. "Suzanne tried. Laura is determined. She says we won't be able to patch things up if you're always around to remind her of what happened."

"But she can't stay mad forever. If we don't flaunt our relationship—"

"Like not showing up at Scott Dunnel's party?" Amy groaned over her own bad joke.

"I'm trying to be serious," he told her with a determined look on his face. "There has to be some way we can work this out with Laura."

"The only thing we can do is wait until she calms down," Amy said. She wanted to believe there was some magical solution, but she knew Laura would find out if they tried to trick her. There was no way she could be with Ben until Laura said it was all right.

"Wait! That's it!"

Hope sparked in Ben's eyes. "You've got the answer?"

"I think so. We can get back together as soon as Laura settles down. When she can forget and forgive, I'll talk to her about us seeing each other again."

"How long will it take?" he asked. "Two days? A week?"

Laura was more stubborn than that, Amy knew. When Laura decided an argument was finally over, then it was never talked about again; but she could take forever to reach that point. She had to be honest with Ben. "It could be a month or more."

"A month?" Ben's hands dropped off her shoulders as if he'd been burned. With a look that said she had to be kidding, he asked, "You expect me to put us *on hold* for a month . . . or more?"

Amy could see he didn't appreciate her idea. She wanted to ask if the magic they'd felt between them wasn't worth waiting for, but she was afraid of his answer.

Ben blinked and ran his hand through his hair distractedly. "I don't understand how all this happened. Amy, how could someone as perfect as you get into a mess this big?"

Perfect? He had thought she was perfect?

Finding out too late that he felt that way about her made Amy sad. "Can you give me a break, Ben?" She held up her hands in a helpless gesture. "I made a mistake. Anyone can do that."

"You want a break?" He pulled hard on his fingers and cracked his knuckles, something Amy had never seen him do before. "What do you want me to do?"

"Wait for me," she whispered, almost afraid to ask. He had already said he wouldn't be a part of that plan, but he meant so much to Amy that she had to try to talk him into it. "Things are going pretty well for Laura. I don't think she'll stay mad too long."

His response to her plea was a sad smile. "I wish it could work, but don't you see it's just one more lie? You want to tell Laura we've broken up when all the time we would just be waiting for her to forget about us."

When he put it that way, it sounded about as honest as the way she'd handled everything else so far. Still, she wanted to hang onto Ben any way she could. "She wouldn't have to know . . ."

"Listen to yourself!" Ben almost yelled at her. "Amy, I care about you. And I care about what could happen for us. But I don't want something built on lies." He reached for his jacket.

"Ben please don't leave," Amy cried in panic.

His arms slid into the sleeves. "There's nothing more to say."

She grabbed his hand as he stood. "It has to end like this?"

He stared at her hand and then her face. She saw only regret in his eyes when he said, "We really don't have any choice."

Ben started toward the door, but Amy stayed on the couch. Standing at the door and watching him drive away into the darkness would only make her feel worse . . . if that was possible.

She curled up, hugging one of the pillows on the couch. How had her life turned upside down in just two weeks? She hadn't wanted to go to the Yellow Dog concert, and she had never set out to hurt her friend's feelings. If she'd been thinking more clearly, she might have handled it better, but Ben had been right when he said there was something magic between them.

She couldn't have told Laura about him before the date, because she wouldn't have turned Ben down even if that's what her friend had wanted. So what could she say about the whole fiasco? Should she have told him to find another history partner? Could she have pretended she was busy the night he had tickets for *South Pacific*? It would have been impossible. She would do it all again if it meant she could spend two more weeks around Ben Richardson. Of all people, Laura Newman should understand that sometimes things happened with guys that just couldn't be explained . . . not even to best friends.

"It looks like you have everything under control," Laura said in the Tylers' basement Friday afternoon.

"I have some cleaning to do tomorrow," Amy admitted. She was glad to have Suzanne's party to keep her busy.

Laura dug into the bag she had brought to Amy's house. "Here are the tapes you wanted. I'll bring over the bags of popcorn tomorrow when it's time to work on the cake."

"That'll be fine." It wasn't as hard to be with Laura as Amy had expected it to be, but she didn't feel much like having a conversation with anyone.

Laura checked her watch. "I can't stay much longer, because I have to get ready for the big party." She rolled her eyes. "I can't believe Mike is taking me to Scott's house tonight!"

"Have enough fun for both of us," Amy said softly while she arranged Laura's tapes on the table.

"I didn't know you were interested in Scott's party," Laura told her with surprise.

"I was supposed to be there with . . ." She couldn't bring herself to say *Ben*.

"You were?" Laura asked in disbelief.

Amy resented her friend acting as though Ben were such a loser he couldn't possibly have been invited to the party. She stared coolly into Laura's eyes. "Yes."

Laura looked confused for just a second. "Hey, I didn't know," she said, easily recovering her poise. "I'll tell you all about it tomorrow while we frost the cake."

Amy followed her friend upstairs to the kitchen, and she stood with her nose pressed against the window after Laura had left. She couldn't help wishing Laura wasn't the only one getting ready for the party right now.

"Are you going to stand there all night?" her mother asked.

"What?" Amy turned and noticed her mother at the stove. Amy knew she'd walked right past her mom and not even seen her. "Can I help with dinner or something?"

"You could set the table."

While she put out the plates and arranged the silverware, Amy thought about the party and Ben. It would have been great. They had never danced together, and he had kissed her only a few times. Thinking about everything she was missing, Amy sank into one of the kitchen chairs.

"I thought we could rent some movies tonight," her mother said.

"Okay," Amy mumbled.

"Then we can stay up half the night watching them while we eat everything in sight." Her mother took a pack of vegetables from the freezer.

"All right."

Mrs. Tyler sat down at the table with her frozen peas and carrots in hand. "Amy, I know it won't be as good as going out with Ben, but won't it be better than sitting up in your room alone thinking about how things could have been?"

Amy looked up with tears in her eyes. "You're great, Mom. What would I do without you?"

"I don't think you'd be eating dinner without my help," she said, pointing to each of the place settings.

Amy noticed the three forks on the place mat where her mother was sitting. There were three spoons in front of her. And her father had three knives. She couldn't help smiling. "What are we having?"

"Pork chops." Her mother smiled at her.

"It would be a little hard cutting any meat with this," she acknowledged, waving a spoon.

"Welcome back to the real world," her mother said. "You might not quite believe it yet, but life is going to go on."

She knew her mother was trying to help, but things weren't that easy. "I know tomorrow will come, and then the next day, and then the next. But it's not going to be the same without Ben."

Chapter Ten

"Just let me test the frosting," Laura begged, trying to grab the small bowl from Amy's hands.

Amy hugged the container close to her body. "You can lick the bowl after we're done with the cake."

Laura's lower lip protruded in a fake pout. "You sound just like my mother."

"Yeah? Well, if only half the cake is covered with frosting, we both know who Suzanne's going to blame," Amy warned. Laura's tasting routine had spoiled last year's cake for that very reason.

"Are you going to remind me of that for the rest of my life?" Laura asked with a sigh, still eyeing the chocolate mixture as Amy spread it over the cake.

"Probably," Amy said.

"Oh, well, I guess I can wait. Things are *so* wonderful," Laura said dreamily. She leaned against the counter. "I just can't tell you what a great time I had last night. You should have been there."

"I would have liked that, too," Amy said under her breath, but not so quietly that Laura didn't hear it.

"Hey, I'm sorry."

Amy knew her friend's apology was genuine. Laura might not feel guilty for breaking up Amy's romance, but she wasn't the kind of person who would purposely try to make her feel worse. "It's okay. I'm surviving."

The conversation died. Amy didn't want to discuss Ben with Laura. She had made her decision, and now she was living with it, but that didn't mean she wanted to talk about it. Apparently Laura felt the same way.

"Tell me more about the party," Amy said finally. She dabbed at the frosting one last time and handed over the bowl.

Laura smiled and ran the spoon around the sides of the bowl. Her eyes lit up as she licked the frosting off the spoon, and then she sighed.

"You want to know about the party? What can I say? Scott lives in a huge house. We partied in the basement . . . but it's nothing like the downstairs in either of our houses. There was a brick fireplace that ran up to the ceiling, and an entertainment system that filled a whole wall. You should have heard Yellow Dog on that machine!"

"So did you dance?"

"Danced, ate, talked. There was a long table full of nachos, chicken wings, barbecued ribs . . . and vegetable strips for the girls on diets."

Amy looked at the chocolate smudging Laura's lips. "Did that include you?"

"Are you kidding? Mike likes a girl who isn't afraid to eat, so I tried everything!"

"He said that?" Amy had never heard that guys liked to watch girls eat.

"Not exactly. But he said he's tired of girls who are obsessed with calorie counting, and Scott agreed. He's sick of being the only one who gets buttered popcorn at the movies."

With both Mike and Scott thinking that way, Amy guessed her friend had taken seconds and thirds on everything. "Ready to write *Happy Birthday* on the cake?"

Laura picked up the frosting tube off the counter and started to work. Amy watched the first word appear on the top of the cake. The party was going to be perfect. If only she could say the same about the rest of her life.

The phone rang, and Amy grabbed the receiver. Could it be— "Hello?"

"Hi. I'm looking for Laura Newman," a guy with a deep, rumbling voice said.

"Laura?" Amy couldn't figure out who was on the other end of the line. It certainly wasn't Laura's dad.

"Her mother told me I could find her at 555-1279." The deep voice sounded a little hesitant.

"Sure. Just a minute." Amy covered the mouthpiece with her hand. "Laura, there's some guy on the phone for you."

Laura mouthed, "A guy?" She wiped her hands on a dish towel and took the receiver. "This is Laura."

Amy wished she could hear what the guy was saying. Laura's dark eyes opened wider than Amy had ever seen them. She hooked her index finger around the phone cord and bounced it while she listened to her caller. Finally she said in a breathy voice, "I'd love to. What time will you pick me up?"

She hung up the phone and stared at it for a full minute. Amy couldn't stand the suspense any longer. "Who was it?"

Laura spun around, eyes sparkling, a huge smile on her face. "Scott Dunnel! Can you believe it!"

"Scott? That was Scott?" Amy couldn't believe she'd talked to him and not realized who it was. Laura had built him up to be so wonderful that Amy felt almost honored that he'd dialed her number. "What did he want?"

Laura pressed her hands to her cheeks as if she were trying to hold in her excitement. "A date!"

"A date?" Amy was beginning to sound like a parrot. But this was like history happening in her own kitchen. Laura had been watching Scott and talking about him since the beginning of their sophomore year. After a year and a half, it was too much to think her friend's dream was coming true. "When?"

"Tonight."

Amy looked at the cake with only half a birthday wish written across it. "*Tonight?*"

She stuffed her hands in her jeans pockets and tried to think. There were ten girls coming to the party, so they couldn't exactly call it off on a few hours' notice; besides, Suzanne had only one birthday a year. She couldn't believe Laura would back out of the party at the last minute. They'd been planning it together for weeks.

"I'm not stupid," Laura said, interrupting Amy's thoughts. "Scott wants to pick me up for the movie in two hours. Obviously his real plans for the night bombed and I was his second choice."

"How do you feel about that?" Normally Laura didn't like coming in second in any kind of competition.

Laura held her head high. "I don't care. This is an opportunity, and I want to take advantage of it."

"Of course." Amy wouldn't hold her friend back from something this important. But how would Suzanne feel? "The party will be okay without you, I guess."

"Do you think so?" Laura asked, distracted.

"Sure."

"Great!" Laura said, already moving toward the door. "Then I've got to go. I only have two hours to get ready for the biggest date in my life!"

"Good luck," Amy called as her friend disappeared through the back door. She watched Laura run through the snow to her house.

"Did Laura leave?" Amy's mother asked, coming into the kitchen. "Is everything ready?"

"No." Amy halfheartedly picked up the frosting tube and held it over the cake.

"Could I finish that for you?" her mother asked.

"Would you? Laura had to leave and I'm so bad at this."

"I remember," her mother said with a laugh. "The last time you tried to write something with frosting it looked like you'd written it in Greek."

Amy filled the sink with foamy water and started washing the pans and bowls they had used to bake the cake.

"How's this?" Her mother stood back so they could both check out her work.

"It's great. I couldn't have done it without you," Amy told her mom.

"What happened to Laura? You two didn't get in a fight about Ben, did you?"

"Laura has a date," Amy said.

"A date? Tonight?" Her mother squinted at Amy. "Am I missing something? I thought you two were throwing a big party here tonight."

"We are . . . or at least I am. It will be fine," Amy said confidently. "Scott Dunnel just called her and she has been absolutely dying for a date with him."

"So she's standing you up for some guy?" her mother asked, staring thoughtfully at her daughter. "Are you sure she's not trying to pay you back for Ben?"

"Mother!" Amy was shocked. "Laura wouldn't do that."

"Okay. I'm sorry." She reached out and touched Amy on the arm. "What else needs to be done?"

"You're going to help me?" Amy needed all the help she could get.

"I know I'm not as much fun as Laura, but I'll do what I can," her mother promised.

"And the next song is for a special girl from Madison High. Happy Birthday, Suzanne!" the disc jockey screamed.

"Me?" Suzanne squealed. "Is he talking about me?"

"He sure is," Amy said with a grin. The party was going just the way she and Laura had planned it.

"How did KWAK know it was my birthday?" Suzanne questioned.

"Laura arranged it." Amy was surprised by the groans that met Laura's name.

"At least she did *something* to help with the party," one girl said cynically.

"Really, you've done a great job without her."

"I still can't believe she stuck you with all the work just because Scott called."

"She always jumps when a guy calls."

Amy turned from person to person as their feelings about Laura were voiced. Their complaints made her very uncomfortable.

"It's really okay with me," Amy said quietly. "I mean, Laura and I talked it over and I'm the one who told her it was all right . . . that I could handle the party myself."

"What else were you going to say?" the girl next to Amy asked. "I can't see you forbidding Laura to leave."

"Can you imagine Amy blocking the door to keep Laura in this house?"

"Or standing over her, making her work while Scott took another girl to the movies?" Suzanne suggested.

The others started laughing, and they couldn't seem to stop. They collapsed on their sleeping bags, consumed with giggles as they imagined Amy standing up to Laura.

"It's not funny," Amy said stubbornly when the laughter subsided enough for her to be heard. "It wasn't like that. Laura's not like that."

"C'mon, Amy. You're just too nice to admit Laura would have sold her own family to get a date with Scott. It wouldn't have mattered if you asked her to stay. Compared to Scott Dunnel, this party isn't worth anything to her."

Amy stuck out her chin. She hated it when they made her sound so good and sweet. "Would any of you have been different?"

"What!" Suzanne shrieked. "Do you think we're all dying for a date with Scott?"

"No." She had to make them see they were being unfair. "Nadine, wouldn't you have passed up a party with us if someone had broken their leg and you had a chance to dance in the Nutcracker Suite?"

Everyone knew how hard Nadine had worked learning several roles in case one of the dancers couldn't have gone on. "I would have gone . . . but you guys would have understood."

"And you, Meg." Amy turned to the girl behind her. "If you had made the finals in that orchestra competition last summer, you wouldn't have worried about missing our big picnic . . ."

Meg shook her head. "You don't get chances like that very often. I couldn't have passed it up."

"That's exactly how Laura felt this afternoon," Amy said, pleased to have proved her point.

"It's not the same," Nadine argued. "A date isn't as important as a performance."

"It is to Laura," Amy argued. "Maybe we don't feel the way about any guys that Laura feels about Scott. But believe me, this is her chance to do something she's been looking forward to for over a year!" Amy looked over at Suzanne, who nodded in agreement.

"I guess we have to believe you. You guys know Laura best," Meg allowed.

"But how can you be such good friends to her after the things she's been saying about you and Ben Richardson?" the girl next to Suzanne asked Amy.

Amy didn't know Laura had been talking about Ben. "What has she been saying?"

"That you met Ben when he was *her* date, and the two of you started sneaking around behind her back."

"She didn't say that," Suzanne argued.

"Maybe those weren't her exact words, but that's what she meant," the other girl insisted.

Amy tried to convince herself it was just one person's interpretation. She couldn't believe Laura would say such mean things about her after she'd given up Ben to save their friendship. Although she didn't like talking about what had happened, she had to set the story straight.

Amy told them about the double date where Laura had been much more involved with Yellow Dog than with Ben, and she tried to describe the magic that happened between Ben and herself. Once she explained how upset Laura had been Sunday morning, they understood why she hadn't hurried to announce the next day that Ben was in her history class.

"But why didn't you tell her when you finally had a date with him?" one of the girls asked.

"I tried to," Amy claimed, but the others looked skeptical. "Okay, maybe I could have tried harder. But the truth is, I wanted to go out with Ben and I knew Laura wouldn't want me to do it."

"I guess that just shows how different you two are." Meg shook her head. "When Laura wanted to go out tonight, you told her to go ahead. But you couldn't tell her about Ben a week ago, because she would have stopped you from going out with someone you like as much as she thinks she likes Scott."

"And now she's broken them up altogether," the girl next to Suzanne moaned.

"That's the price I had to pay for keeping a secret. It's my fault," Amy said, convinced she had caused her own problems.

"Give us a break, Tyler," Nadine complained. "Laura was unfair . . . in fact, she was downright mean to you. Why can't you see that?"

"You're wrong." Amy didn't like confessing her mistakes to everyone, but she had to make them understand. "I betrayed Laura's trust. She was hurt. I don't like how things turned out, but I don't blame her."

"You're too good to be real," one girl tried to say, but Amy covered her ears.

"Amy can't help the way she is," Suzanne

said, giving her a hug. "I just think Laura's lucky to have a friend like her."

"Maybe Laura's lucky, but I feel sorry for Ben and Amy. It sounds like they really had something special between them."

"We almost did," Amy said, her voice dangerously close to breaking. She felt a little better, knowing the other girls didn't blame her the way Laura had done. Still, their sympathy didn't fill the empty place in her heart.

"I know what this party needs," Suzanne declared after a few moments of silence. "Pizza!"

It took them twenty minutes to decide how many pizzas to order and what to have on them. By the time they had placed the order and requested a cute delivery man, Laura's desertion and Amy's sad heart were almost forgotten. But when the girls flipped through the channels to find some good videos and passed over the movie version of *South Pacific*, Amy had to wonder what Ben was doing at that moment. How long was it going to take her to get over him?

Chapter Eleven

Amy finally found Ben leaning against a locker, reading a book. She had choked down her chicken patty and salad when she saw him leave the lunchroom early. She guessed he had gone up to their history class, and she was right. Apparently Mr. Wilson was enjoying his usual long lunch in the teacher's lounge; the classroom door was closed and locked.

Talking about Ben at the slumber party had left her sorry they had parted on such bad terms. He hadn't even said goodbye. If one more thing could happen between them, Amy wanted them still to be some kind of friends.

"Hi, Ben," she called.

He looked up with a stony expression on his face. "Hello."

His cold look didn't make her feel very welcome, and for a moment her brain was a blank. It certainly wouldn't be a good idea to ask him how things were going. If he felt half as lonely as she did, his day wasn't going very well.

"Did you go to Scott's party?" she asked, not sure how safe that subject was either.

"No" he said gruffly. "I filled in for a guy at the station."

"Did they finally let you run one of the cameras for the Friday night news or what?" She thought a little joke might make him relax.

He hooked his left thumb through a belt loop. "Look, Amy. I don't really feel like talking. That's why I came up here to be alone."

"I'm sorry." He didn't have to sound so crabby. Did he think she'd searched for him just so she could annoy him?

"Sorry for what?" he asked pointedly.

The angry spark in his eyes dampened her hopes for smoothing things over with him. "I guess I'm sorry for lots of things."

He snapped the book shut and closed his eyes as if he were trying to gather his thoughts. Finally he asked, "What do you want from me?"

"I'd like to be friends," she said shyly.

"Friends?" He stared at her in utter surprise.

Amy tried not not to be discouraged by his reaction. "Maybe it's more like acquaintances," she said, using one of her mother's words. "I don't see why we can't be friendly when we run into each other around school."

"You mean you want me to stop by your table in the lunchroom to ask how your day is going? If I run into you at the concession stand at a basketball game, should I buy you a Coke? What do you want me to do, Amy Tyler?"

"I want you not to hate me," she said honestly. "I care about you, Ben. I know the situation that came between us was my fault—"

"A situation! Is *that* what you call it?" He clenched his jaw, then pressed his palm against his forehead. "I can't be one of your friends. I'm sorry if that hurts your feelings, but every time I see you, I feel like I'm being kicked in the stomach. I'd be a fool to be involved with you in any way."

His blunt explanation sobered Amy. He had been hurt even more deeply than she realized. Although she had lost him, she'd held on to her best friend. What had been left for Ben?

"Do you want to call off the history project?" she asked, not wanting to force him to do anything that would make him feel worse.

"Our presentation is scheduled for Wednesday. How can we quit now?"

"I guess we can't." What argument could they give Mr. Wilson for canceling two days before their report was due? "Is your part ready?"

"Yes."

She noticed he didn't ask how far she was on her half of the project. "I still need a little more information on the battle," she offered.

He squatted and unzipped the backpack he had left on the floor. Without looking up at her, he handed over a book. "I found this very helpful."

"Thanks." She took it, being very careful not to touch his hand. "I'll give it back to you in class tomorrow."

"You don't need to do that."

"I don't mind," she insisted. Amy understood why he didn't want to see her anymore, but she wasn't going to fall off the face of the earth. They would be in the same history class for the rest of the quarter.

"You don't have to give it back to me. I'm done with it. Just return it to the library," he said in a businesslike tone.

"Okay."

The lunch period was almost over, and the hall was starting to get crowded. She tried to

146

think of something else to say to Ben; something that might make him feel a little better, but he didn't seem to need her concern. As soon as some guys arrived for class, Ben asked them what they thought about the university hockey team's big win over the weekend. He didn't look back at her even once.

"Can we talk?" Laura asked urgently when she stopped by Amy's locker after school.

Amy sighed. "Sure. Is the Tiger's Den all right?" She threw Ben's history book into her backpack along with her other homework for the next day.

"Not really."

Amy looked up in surprise. "No? What would the Tiger's Den do without our business?"

"Okay," Laura said quickly. "But can we get a table in the back . . . *alone*?"

Amy took a closer look at her friend. Laura was chewing her lower lip, ruining her always perfect lipstick. "What's wrong? Is it something about Scott?"

"Scott's fine," Laura replied without the enthusiasm she usually had when she mentioned his name.

"Then what is it?"

"Get your stuff and we'll talk there."

Laura filled their block and a half walk to the Tiger's Den with the details on the disaster in her chemistry class. The class brain had blown up a test tube and the teacher had gone crazy. If her friend hadn't acted so strangely at the locker, Amy would have thought this was just a regular afternoon for the two of them.

They quickly ordered something to drink, and then Laura got down to what was on her mind. "I heard that everyone was talking about me at Suzanne's party."

"You did?" If Amy had already had her drink, she would have choked on it. A lot of uncomplimentary things had been said about Laura that night. Is that what she had heard?

"They really trashed me . . ."

"Some people were surprised you weren't at the party," Amy explained. "It hurt them to think you'd deserted us all for Scott." If Laura understood the motives behind the comments, maybe she wouldn't take them as badly.

"Don't be nice, Amy. People were careful to repeat the conversation word for word. They criticized me . . . and you defended me. Thanks."

Amy shrugged. "No problem. That's what friends are for."

Laura held up her hands. "Stop. I have more to say."

The waitress delivered two large Cokes, and Amy took a long sip of hers, waiting for Laura to continue. Her friend stirred the ice chips in her drink, apparently stalling for time.

Finally, she said, "I've been thinking a lot since everyone started talking to me about Saturday night. We had a whole party to coordinate, but you didn't hesitate for a second when Scott called. You just wanted me to go and have a good time."

"What else could I do?" Amy didn't see anything heroic about what she had done Saturday afternoon. "You'd been waiting for that night to happen for over a year!"

"But three days before, I had thrown a fit because you were seeing Ben. How could you be so nice to me after I'd torn you two apart? Compared to you, I don't look like much of a friend."

"Don't say that." If Laura hadn't been a special friend, Amy never would have given up Ben for her. "Your friendship is important to me."

Laura shook her head so furiously that her slicked-back hair actually moved. "What kind of friend could be so mean when she knows her friend likes a certain guy? You weren't hurting anyone, but it didn't matter to me—"

"Your pride was hurt," Amy said, defending Laura.

"Pride," she snorted. "I was only thinking about myself. I never was interested in Ben, so what did it matter to me whether or not you dated him?"

"Are you saying you were wrong?" Amy pulled her straw out of her glass and pretended to study it. She didn't want to think how different things would be right now if Laura had only realized this last week.

"Wrong. Selfish. You pick the word you want." Laura sounded miserable. "I want you and Ben to get back together."

Amy dropped the straw and Coke dribbled on the table. "That's not possible."

"What?" Laura pulled a napkin from the rack and soaked up the spilled liquid. "I thought you guys had some hot romance."

"It was *very* special." Amy wanted to explain how it had almost seemed magical, but it would probably sound stupid. "Unfortunately, he's made it very clear he never wants to see me again."

"If you had something so great between you, why did he give up so easily?" Laura asked.

150

"I guess he believed me when I told him I couldn't see him anymore." Amy didn't think she had to remind Laura how she had come to that decision.

"So? If you were that special to him, he should have tried to work things out."

In her mind, Amy saw the scene in her living room where Ben had tried to convince her the breakup wasn't necessary. The memory was so clear it brought tears to her eyes. "He did try," she said in a husky voice. Amy coughed and continued, "Ben wanted to find a way for us to keep seeing each other, but I knew you wouldn't agree. I suggested we put our relationship on hold until it would be okay with you for us to start seeing each other again."

"And it's fine with me, so give him a call."

Amy shifted uncomfortably in her seat. What she had to tell Laura wasn't going to ease her friend's conscience. "You don't understand. He hated the idea. Ben said it would be another lie because I would be letting you believe things were over when they really weren't, and he wouldn't settle for a relationship built on lies."

Amy kept part of the story to herself. If Ben had known it would take less than a week, he might have waited for her. They just would have had to skip one weekend of dating. It seemed like every day something new happened that made the problem more complicated and more depressing. With her luck, Ben would have a new girlfriend by the end of the week.

Laura sighed deeply. "All this talk about lies and relationships surprises me. I didn't think he was such a serious guy."

"I got the impression he'd been burned before by girls who played games." It hurt, but Amy had to face the facts. "As it turned out, I guess I fit right into that category."

"You? You're the straightest person I know."

"That just shows how strange this whole thing is." Amy appreciated her friend's support. After all, she had never intended to keep secrets from either Ben or Laura.

"Is there *anything* I can do for you?" Laura's eyes were dark with regret. "I could try to fix you up with someone for Friday. That way, you wouldn't be just sitting around the house feeling bummed."

"Please, no," Amy cried. "I'm not ready for you to do that to me again."

"I'm going to be seeing a lot of Scott, and I hate to think of you staying home alone because I single-handedly wrecked your romance."

"I'll be okay," Amy said dully.

"What about Ben? He didn't look too good when I saw him in the hall today."

"Just seeing me makes him upset," she told her friend.

"Wow. Are you still doing that history thing with him?"

"Wednesday." Amy shuddered to think how much better she'd do on her presentation if Ben would come over to her house tomorrow night just to run through it. Instead she was going to be a bundle of nerves. Facing the class would be bad enough, but doing it with a Ben who wouldn't even look at her was going to be a guaranteed disaster. "After lunch, I'll be General Beauregard and he'll be General McDowell and we'll each tell our sides of the story of Bull Run."

"Who won?"

"You're as bad at history as I am!" Amy exclaimed. "Beauregard's side won. Or at least that's how it's supposed to turn out. Who knows what will happen Wednesday?"

"Are you going to let Ben rewrite history?"

Amy laughed in spite of herself. If Ben were even half as distracted as she was going to be, anything could happen. At least until they did the report, Ben couldn't completely ignore her. Sudden inspiration made her gasp. "Do you think I could find a way to let him know things are better between you and me?" she whispered.

"You mean during your debate?" Laura's eyes lit up with the challenge.

"It's not a debate. I'd have to find a way to work it into my report." Amy bit her longest nail while she gave it some thought. The way Ben had left things today, he probably wouldn't even listen if she tried to tell him the disaster was over . . . not that she would chase him around school and blurt out the news in the middle of a busy hallway.

"I'll help you," Laura volunteered.

"Can you come over tonight?" She could show Laura her outline for her talk and they could look for a place where she could sneak a double meaning into her report.

"I feel terrible about this mess. I'll be there."

Chapter Twelve

"Oh no!" Suzanne cried in distress. "She's eating hot caramel sundaes!"

"Why didn't you wait for us?" Laura asked.

Amy looked up from the booth at the Tiger's Den where she was sitting alone that Wednesday afternoon. She pointed to the nearly eaten sundae with her spoon. "I thought this would make me feel better."

Suzanne slid onto the bench across from Amy and glared at the empty ice-cream dish in front of her. "Either no one cleaned this table before you sat down, or you're already on your second sundae."

"Yeah. It's my second and my third should be here any second," Amy muttered.

Laura scooted in next to Suzanne. "We all

know you turn to hot caramel sundaes when facing disaster . . . but three? I've never seen you have more than two!"

"Are you failing a class?" Suzanne asked.

Amy scraped the last bits of caramel out of her dish. "No. I'm doing fine in my classes—even history."

"History!" Laura smacked herself on the forehead. "Today was the presentation. How did it go?"

"It all depends . . ." The waitress delivered the third sundae and picked up the two empty bowls. Amy sank her spoon into the goo.

"What do you mean 'it depends'?" Laura asked impatiently.

"Are you asking about my grade or Ben?" Amy inquired between bites.

"We want to know about Ben, of course," Suzanne replied.

"I did just what we planned," she started. Monday night both Laura and Suzanne had helped her plant a secret message in her report. "When I got to the part where I told how the Union thought by noon that they had won the battle, I looked Ben straight in the eyes and said: *But it wasn't over yet. They should have known things can change.*" Amy paused for a few more bites of her sundae.

"It sounds like you did it just the way we planned," Laura observed. "Didn't he get the message?"

"He blinked twice and I thought he caught the hint, but when it was his turn to say his part, he didn't try to answer me or anything."

"Is that all that's bothering you?" Laura laughed. "Amy, it took us hours to find a way to fit the news into your presentation. Did you expect him to figure out how to answer you in the few minutes he had before he did his part of the report?"

"It wasn't just that," Amy said sadly. "When the bell rang, Mr. Wilson asked us to stay after class so he could discuss our grade. When he finished, Ben and I were alone. I kinda blocked the door so he couldn't leave."

"You didn't!" Suzanne's eyes sparkled at the thought.

"I shouldn't have wasted the energy," Amy said bitterly. "I said I had something to tell him, and he said he wasn't stupid. He'd gotten my hidden message."

"So he knows I want you two to get back together." Laura sighed with relief, as if her conscience were finally clear.

Amy shook her head. "Before I could tell him what had happened, he told me he didn't want

to hear about my latest scam. Then he left."
She sighed. "It really is over between us."

"Don't be so pessimistic," Laura scolded.

Amy plunged her spoon into the center of her
sundae so it stood up straight. "What do you
expect me to do? Ben can't stand the sight of
me, and he doesn't believe anything I say. It's
time for me to forget about him."

"And gain forty pounds while you're trying to
erase the memories." Laura grabbed the sundae bowl and put it on the empty table next to
them. "Feeling sorry for yourself isn't going to
help."

"You sound like a mom," Amy complained.

"It's my mother's favorite line." Laura grinned.
"But I think you need it."

"Cheer up," Suzanne said, forcing a smile.
"At least one good thing must have happened
today."

"Sure. I got an A minus on my history project."

Both Suzanne's and Laura's mouths dropped
open. Together they asked, "An A minus?"

"Yeah." Amy rested her chin in her hands.
"What a joke. I agreed to be Ben's partner because I thought it was a way for me to finally do
well in history. But now I couldn't care less
about the grade."

Amy stared at the remains of her last sundae

melting on the next table. Then she turned her sad gaze on her friends.

"We have to do something," Suzanne whispered to Laura.

"Hang in there," Laura told Amy. "We're going to help you survive this thing."

"You're not wearing that!" Laura made a face that Amy had only seen once before . . . when Laura tried to eat spinach.

"If you don't like it, then I'll just stay home," Amy said stubbornly.

Laura clapped her hands to her head. "You can't!"

"Why not? You know I hate blind dates, and I hate double dates. Especially now. I'd rather stay home and do my math assignment."

"You have all day tomorrow to do your homework. It's Saturday night, and Scott is picking both of us up in twenty minutes." Laura went to Amy's open closet and sorted through her clothes.

Amy lay on her bed, crossing her legs at the ankles. She knew her friend was trying to help, but she was getting tired of having Laura and Suzanne fussing over her. The last thing she needed was another date arranged by Laura. She hadn't recovered from the last one yet.

"Try this," Laura suggested, pulling a pair of black wool slacks off its hanger.

"Fine." Amy swung her legs off the bed and took the pants from her friend. She climbed out of her jeans and stepped into the pants. "Are you happy now?"

Laura stepped back for a better view and covered her mouth to hold back her giggles. "The sweatshirt doesn't do much for it. Where's your pink sweater? The one with the embroidered flowers?"

"On the shelf," Amy said, pointing to the top of her closet. If Laura wanted to dress her, then she could do all the work. She took off the sweatshirt and threw it on her bed. When she saw Laura undoing the bottons on the sweater, Amy protested. "I can put it on myself."

"Then do it. We have to hurry."

The phone rang while Amy was getting into the sweater. Her mother called up the stairs, "Amy, it's for you. Suzanne."

"There's no time," Laura mumbled. "Let me do your hair while you talk."

Amy put the receiver to her ear and let Laura worry about how she was going to brush her hair. What was wrong with the way it was, anyway? "Hi, Suzanne."

"How's it going?" Suzanne asked. "Ready for your date?"

"I thought I was until Laura decided to do a make-over on me," Amy complained. "Just because she looks great in her leather miniskirt, she thinks I have to dress up, too."

"You want to look good, don't you?" Suzanne wondered.

"Why? Blind dates always bomb. I don't care what he thinks of me."

"You might tonight," Suzanne said mysteriously.

"What's that supposed to mean?"

"Nothing," Suzanne said quickly. "You just never know what's going to happen. Maybe the guy will be a hunk."

"Maybe he will, but I've gotta go," Amy said urgently. "Now Laura's digging in my jewelry box. I have to stop her before she has me more dressed up than Princess Di!"

"I'm just looking for your dangly pearl earrings," Laura said innocently when Amy hung up the phone. "Here they are!"

While Amy put in the earrings, her friend peered at her face. "What's wrong with me now?" Amy wanted to know.

"You need some eyeshadow."

"It's in the bathroom." Amy started for the door.

"Never mind." Laura grabbed her purse off the bed. "I've got some in here."

"You're more prepared than any Boy Scout I've ever met," Amy teased. Laura was acting so weird that Amy couldn't stay grumpy. Her friend was too funny.

"Close your eyes," Laura instructed.

"Can I look yet?" Amy asked when her friend finally stopped smudging the shadow on her eyelids.

"Finished," Laura said dramatically.

Amy had to look twice into the mirror. She had to admit Laura had done a good job.

"Now all you need is lipstick." Laura picked up a tube from the dresser.

Amy grabbed for it at the same time and nearly had to wrestle Laura to get it away from her. "If you don't mind, I can do this myself."

The doorbell rang downstairs just as Amy blotted her lips.

"Ready?" Laura asked with a grin on her face.

"Ready for *nothing*," Amy said, following her friend down the stairs.

Amy's father whistled when she came down the stairs. "It must be a big date. You look great."

"Cut it out, Dad." Amy blushed, embarrassed to have Scott Dunnel hear her father fussing over her.

"Really, Amy. You look all right," Scott called from the entryway where Laura was whispering in his ear.

Amy nearly choked. Scott Dunnel was complimenting *her*? All she needed was another date of Laura's paying too much attention to her.

"We should hit the road," Scott told the girls. "Amy's date is waiting at the restaurant."

On the way to the Parker Inn, Amy tried to get Scott or Laura to say something about her date. Was he a senior? They wouldn't tell her. Was he tall or short? Scott said he was about medium. Was he cute? Laura replied looks were a matter of taste.

It didn't make much sense to Amy. Either they were trying to keep a secret or the guy was a real dog. Maybe they just believed blind dates should stay a mystery until the two people met. She chose to think Scott and Laura enjoyed the intrigue, because her best friend wouldn't have set her up with a loser, not after all she had been through lately.

Scott and Laura walked into the restaurant lobby ahead of Amy. Since she was the shortest one, she couldn't see a thing.

"There he is," Scott called, waving to someone across the lobby.

"Where's *my* date?" the mystery man asked, and Amy's heart stopped. The voice sounded too familiar. She had to be imagining things.

Laura stepped aside and said, "She's right here."

Ben's mouth fell open when he saw Amy. He didn't say anything, and she knew why. How could they do this to her? Ben had made it perfectly clear he'd be happy if she moved to China.

"Laura," Amy whispered between gritted teeth. "This isn't going to work." She loved her friend for trying to get them back together, but it would be best if everyone realized right away that it was a big mistake.

"You guys need to talk," Laura said to both of them.

Ben stood in the same spot in stony silence. Scott slapped him on the shoulder. "Loosen up. We're not leaving until you give her a chance."

Amy felt a flutter of hope. If there were going to be a chance for them, this might be it.

"What does this mean?" Ben finally asked, nodding toward Laura.

"It means I was a fool and a rotten person." Laura glanced at Scott, and he gave her a reassuring smile. "I'd feel a lot better if you made up with Amy, but I know that might not be possible. But you can still talk to her and come to some understanding."

Amy was surprised to hear Laura being so logical. She wondered if she'd gotten it from Suzanne or if Scott had been advising her. Of course she would love to patch things up with Ben, but Laura was right. That might not happen. If it couldn't be, she'd feel better if they could at least talk things over one more time.

"I don't have anything else planned for tonight," Ben said, committing himself to nothing.

"Neither do I." Amy struggled to stay as cool as he seemed to be.

"Good." Scott put his arm around Laura's shoulder. "We have a reservation somewhere else, but you two can stay here."

When they left, Amy knew her ride home had just disappeared. If she and Ben didn't come to some kind of terms, she'd have to call her parents. She didn't have enough money in her purse for a taxi.

"Laura must be feeling pretty guilty," Ben said, his hands buried in the pockets of his bomber jacket. "How did it happen?"

"It's a long story." She inched closer to him.

"Could I have the short version?"

She wondered if that meant he didn't plan to stick around long. "I had a chance to keep her from dating Scott, but I didn't try to stop her—even though it meant her backing out of a surprise party we'd been planning for weeks. I didn't do it to prove a point or anything, but it made her realize she'd been wrong about us. Now her conscience bothers her every time she sees me looking miserable."

"You've been miserable?" There was a cautious light in his eyes, as though he were half expecting a trick.

"Terrible," Amy told him. "And you?"

"About the same." He unzipped his jacket, and Amy hoped it meant he was willing to stay for a while. "What do you think we should do about it?"

Amy looked into his eyes. She wasn't sure she should tell him what was really in her heart, but what was she saving it for? If she didn't say it now, she might never have another chance. "I'd like to think we could be together again . . . like we were before."

He pulled one hand out of its pocket and touched her left shoulder. "You want to go back to that mess of secrets and lies?"

She had gambled and lost. Amy told herself not to be too upset. She had done her best. "I guess not."

"Right. I think we should start over completely and forget all that junk in our past."

Amy's heart thudded rapidly with sudden hope. "Are you serious?"

"Why not?" He shrugged his shoulders. "I mean Scott and Laura worked hard to get us together. We might as well give it a try."

"I did give Laura a bad time tonight," she admitted with a shy smile.

"You, too? I told Scott to forget it; I didn't need a date."

Amy looked at the floor. "But now what do you think?"

"I'm glad I came," he whispered in her ear.

"Me, too."

"Excuse me," someone behind Ben said. "How many are there in your party?"

Ben and Amy gazed past the hostess into the fancy restuarant. "Would you rather stay here or go to Torelli's where we can both squeeze into the same side of the booth?" he asked her softly.

"The booth." The mere thought left Amy breathless.

"Sorry," he told the hostess. "We'll be back here another night."

With an arm wrapped around her, Ben pulled Amy close. She snuggled against him as they walked out to his car, not quite sure she wasn't dreaming. She had given up all hope of ever being in Ben's arms again.

"This is too good to be true," she whispered when they found his car.

"It's real," he promised.

"Pinch me, then maybe I'll believe it," she teased.

"I've got a better idea." Ben placed a hand on each side of her face and stared at her intently for a moment. Then he leaned forward to kiss her.

Amy's arms flew around his neck the moment his lips touched hers.

"I think I should stop knocking the idea of blind dates," she said once she got her breath back.

Ben placed a finger over her lips. "Don't talk like that, Amy Tyler. It's going to be a long time before you'll need another blind date."

We hope you enjoyed reading this book. If you would like to receive further information about available titles in the Bantam series, just write to the address below, with your name and address: Kim Prior, Bantam Books, 61–63 Uxbridge Road, Ealing, London W5 5SA

If you live in Australia or New Zealand and would like more information about the series, please write to:

Sally Porter
Transworld Publishers
(Australia) Pty Ltd
15–23 Helles Avenue
Moorebank
NSW 2170
AUSTRALIA

Kiri Martin
Transworld Publishers (NZ) Ltd
Cnr. Moselle and Waipareira Avenues
Henderson
Auckland
NEW ZEALAND

All Bantam and Young Adult books are available at your bookshop or newsagent, or can be ordered at the following address: Corgi/Bantam Books, Cash Sales Department, PO Box 11, Falmouth, Cornwall, TR10 9EN.

Please list the title(s) you would like, and send together with a cheque or postal order. You should allow for the cost of book(s) plus postage and packing charges as follows:

80p for one book
£1.00 for two books
£1.20 for three books
£1.40 for four books
Five or more books free.

Please note that payment must be made in pounds sterling; other currencies are unacceptable.

(The above applies to readers in the UK and Republic of Ireland only)

BFPO customers, please allow for the cost of the book(s) plus the following for postage and packing: 80p for the first book, and 20p per copy for each additional book.

Overseas customers, please allow £1.50 for postage and packing for the first book, £1.00 for the second book, and 30p for each subsequent title ordered.

It's hot! It's sexy! It's fun!

Baby's life changes forever when she meets Johnny. For he is an electrifying dancer, and he shows Baby what dancing is *really* all about – the heat, the rhythm and the excitement . . .

A sensational series based on the characters from the top-grossing *Dirty Dancing* movie and television series.